Baker's Crossing

Dan DeKoning

DEDICATION

I was in the middle of writing this book when I received news that a friend of mine had passed away from complications of Lyme disease.

This book is for you, Jenny.

Baker's Crossing

CHAPTER ONE

The first thing I learned when the world started to fall apart was that I didn't know shit about shit.

You would have thought I would have known something. After all, in the corporate world, I *had* been a big deal. I was the vice president of the human resources department at a huge investment and accounting firm in the city of Charlotte. I had the fate of over three hundred employees at my fingertips, and everyone knew it. Yes, I lived the good life. I had a corner office on the top floor of the twenty-story building, with my own attached bathroom and my assigned parking spot in the executive parking garage in the building's basement. I had a high, six-figure salary, and stock options to boot. You would have thought that I might be one of those pretentious pricks that everyone complains about at happy hour, but that wasn't the case with me. Everyone liked me. I made it a point every day to sit with people in the cafeteria over the lunch hour and find out about their lives and hopes and dreams. It was a goal of mine to meet everyone on staff, and I kept a spreadsheet with everyone's name on it and as I met them, I tracked things like birthdays and company anniversaries and such. Granted, I could have looked up the information in the personnel records, but I genuinely enjoyed hearing people's stories and getting to know them. I even instituted a rule that allowed everyone to wear blue jeans on Fridays. People revered me for that.

Then the shit storm blew in like a harsh winter, and the catastrophes started piling on top of each other like cars at the demolition derby. Let me try to remember how it all fell apart.

First came the global pandemic that our government severely mishandled. Those initially in power thought it was going to be just like the flu and that a person would develop the sniffles combined with a headache, and in seventy-two hours, they'd find themselves cured, but it took little more than an Internet browser and access to an international news source to see that was wrong. Since America had divided itself down party lines for so long, each party picked a side to fall on. One side wanted to follow the science; one side wanted to follow… Well, I'm not quite sure. Anti-science? Is there such a thing as anti-science? Witchcraft maybe? Although I believe witches used a lot of herbs and stuff in their spells, so there was probably a basis of science in that, too.

It was a Belgian entertainment reporter, of all people, who originally broke the first story of what would become the biggest news event of the twenty-first century. She was on assignment in South America, following a musician-turned-environmentalist around the jungle when they happened upon a village on the verge of extinction from clear-cutting in the Amazon. The native people put up a good fight, but then tribe members started getting sick, and they passed it off to the foresters, and the foresters took it out of the Amazon and back to their homes in Brazil, or Peru, or Bolivia and passed it on to family members. It didn't take long for the virus to find out that it loved a human host, and it thrived there. By the time the western world took notice, the virus, dubbed the Brazilian Bombshell, had spread throughout South and Central America. Nations recommended their citizens return home, so the previously mentioned reporter got on a plane back to Brussels. She had no symptoms, but she carried the virus with her to Europe, and she wasn't the only one. Thanks to the airplane, the virus spread like wildfire throughout the world. Well, certainly you know the story. Some countries shut down completely and closed their borders, and some didn't. Here, we had a mix. Some people acted responsibly, wore masks, took vaccines, played it safe. Other people said 'fuck it' like they were going to hit the blackjack table in Las Vegas and bet the mortgage, the college funds, and the retirement money all on one hand. Some in the government wanted life to go on as usual, if for the good of the economy, even if at the time upward of sixty percent of the population came down sick.

It took five years for the virus to burn itself out, and it took just over sixty-eight million people with it in this country alone. Other countries fared even worse and lost over seventy percent of their people. Australia came out the winner since they locked down the country immediately and didn't let a plane land or a ship touch its shores until the pandemic was over. Even today, anyone wanting to enter that country must isolate on a ship offshore for three weeks before entering.

After the pandemic subsided and the dead got dealt with, society started to get back to the way things were, and things were fine for a while until the poles started melting at a serious rate. Climate change in America was another one of those two sides of the coin issues. Again, half the people in the country felt it was an important issue, the other half thought it was a hoax. They believed in the Easter Bunny, but not climate change. When an ice shelf the size of Manhattan broke off of Antarctica, it barely made the news. When the ice melted in the Arctic, economists and businesspeople loved the new shorter shipping lanes. And when it rained instead of snowed over Greenland, practically no one noticed. The scientists noticed, of course, but the politicians didn't take it seriously since to them, a degree or two of rising temperature or an inch or two of rising water didn't seem like a big deal. Then hurricane Stephanie blew across the Florida Keys and sent a wall of water into Miami that never quite receded. The rising tides displaced millions of people along both coasts of Florida and the Gulf of Mexico. A reverse migration happened, and rather than retire to Florida or Texas, people moved out to North Dakota and Iowa. If you want to visit Miami Beach these days, you need a snorkel to do it.

Once the seas rose and coastal cities could no longer hold a large number of people, they moved inward to the plains states. Omaha tripled, then quadrupled in size, and Oklahoma City grew from the largest city in Oklahoma to the largest city in the central United States. Of course, the influx of people from the coast caused another problem, and that was where to put them. Cities and towns needed to expand, and that meant farmland got plowed under at an astonishing rate until President Peterson put an end to that with an executive order that limited the amount of acreage that a non-farmer could own. At first, people got angered by that, but when bread and canned beans started to appear on grocery shelves again, the anger subsided.

Although she had the right ideas about the best way to rebound the country, President Peterson served only one term and lost her reelection bid to President Trenton, who was the last president before the country collapsed completely. President Trenton gained a following when he stripped off most of the Conservative party, promising a renewed dedication to the American values of God, guns, and freedom. Even though we had never lost our guns, could still worship whatever god we wanted, or no god at all, and still had as much freedom as we did in 1776. Although President Trenton and his underlings screamed from the rooftops that America was falling into socialism and communism, they themselves were authoritarians, and that was fine with their followers. As long as they were in charge, and they rigged the game so they would be in charge for a long time. Those at the top only craved two things: money and power, and they did all they could to make sure they'd have a never-ending supply of both. The first thing they did was shrink the size of the Supreme Court, stripped it from thirteen justices way back to five, and it just so happened that those five judges were ones under Trenton's thumb. You may wonder how with a lifetime appointment, eight judges would all leave the bench in a year, but again, it came down to money and power. The three most liberal justices all came down with cases of bad luck, and each was involved in untimely, but fatal, accidents. The other five decided to 'retire' to pursue 'other interests'. One brave reporter from a Washington newspaper smelled something rotten, did some digging, and learned that each of the retired justices had each received enough money to last several lifetimes. The newspaper refused to print the story, so the reporter posted it online. It only took fifteen minutes for the website he posted on to suffer a complete failure, and an hour later, someone found the reporter dead in an alley.

Once the court was in his grasp, Trenton's people in Congress headed to work. They decided for the good of election security that elections needed to be tightened, and the way to do that was to go back to the country's founding document, the Constitution. Since the original document provided no one the right to vote, Congress, with a wink and a nod, sent all voting decisions back to the states. Since more than half of the states were flag-waving Trenton lovers, the state governments threw as many people off the voting rolls as they could by going back to their original state charters, and that in turn meant that in most states the only people allowed to vote were white men who owned property. Of course, civil rights groups by the hundreds filed lawsuits, most of which boiled up to the Supreme Court. The Court initially played along and took the cases before siding for the State, but then stopped taking the voting rights cases all together.

Losing a right that only a third of the people used anyway angered a good many fine Americans, and the protests started. Congress, in the name of safety and national security, was in session taking a hard look at the right to assemble when the news broke that Russia had invaded.

For the few years before Russia decided taking on America would be a good idea, they had been busy waging war on their neighbors in an attempt to rebuild the old Soviet Empire. Although the United States didn't get directly involved, they did supply Russia's adversaries with an unending supply of money and weapons, making it hard for Russia to get the quick victories it wanted. So, Russia decided to go for the throat.

Russia went with a two-pronged surprise attack that brought their troops to the west coast and up through Mexico with the plan of taking over half of America before the other half knew what was happening. The Russians lost that war in short order. Not only were they overextended from having to occupy the countries they had recently taken, but they also underestimated not only the greatness of the American military but also the number of gun-toting, freedom-loving good old boys in every back burg of America. I actually felt sorry for the Russians coming in from Mexico. Not only did they have to trudge through the desert in the middle of summer, but by the time they crossed the border, thousands of patriots and soldiers had amassed and sat in air-conditioned pickup trucks waiting for them. Not a single foreign invader made it through that gauntlet. Of course, Russia threatened us all with nukes, and near the end of the war, they actually tried to use them. What they hadn't counted on was the bravery of one Russian general, who, when ordered to fire the nuke, rerouted it for the Russian central command building instead of the White House. It wasn't a large bomb, but big enough to take down the remains of the Russian Empire, and Russia surrendered to America the next day. The best part was, for reparations, NATO forced Russia to give land to the countries they had absorbed. Map lines got redrawn and all the countries that bordered Russia doubled in size. Estonia took control of St. Petersburg and Azerbaijan claimed all the land north to Volgograd. Finland stretched its borders east all the way to the White Sea, and Ukraine claimed Moscow. Kazakhstan moved north, and Mongolia took all the land to the northern shores of Lake Baikal. Even Japan got some long-disputed islands back in the Sea of Okhotsk. When all got said and done, the once-largest country in the world was only a fifth of its former size, and they formed the new Russian capital in Yakutsk.

After the war ended, things in this country got really bad. Prices shot up, inflation rose, and wages dropped like a rock. Even the people who had voted President Trenton and his ilk into office had enough, and protests started overtaking the country like dandelion fields popping up after the spring rains. The working class of the entire country went on a general strike, and practically every business shut down. Thousands of protesters turned up at the state capitols of every state, and in response, President Trenton broke the Posse Comitatus Act and sent the military in to deal with the protesters, which ended up with thousands of Americans dead. The president then declared Marshall Law and canceled the upcoming presidential election, which also didn't go over well, and the protests widened. It's said that four million people marched on Washington, which I can neither confirm nor deny, since all I saw was pictures of the aftermath. The capital city fell, burning and in ruins, and anyone involved in the administration of President Trenton, including Trenton himself, suffered the ultimate consequence. The United States of America had fallen, and all it took was the mismanagement and greed of one madman and his followers.

I saw it all coming because I had an excellent view from my office. It didn't take a financial genius to see the market was going to crash, and it crashed hard. My firm, including myself, got wiped out overnight. I found out I was out of a job when I got to the office one morning and found access to the parking garage blocked, and a note on the front door that said some nonsense about the firm being closed indefinitely, which everyone knew was bullshit. Well, at least I didn't have to wear a tie anymore.

When Washington fell, anarchy descended on the country like nightfall. Even though I lived in the suburbs of Charlotte, I could hear gunfire and sirens around me constantly. I knew I had to get away, find a place to hide out and lie low until someone got things back into some semblance of order.

I had gotten as far as laying out my suitcases on the bed and was deciding what to pack when the doorbell rang. Rather than rush right down and throw open the door, I crept like a thief into the spare bathroom across the hall. Just over the toilet was a window that offered a view of the landing below. I could tell by the top of the head it was my neighbor, Barry.

The doorbell rang again just as I reached to open the door. It was Barry, and he looked different, nervous, scared.

"Hey, Bar, what's going on?" I asked as if it were just a normal Saturday, and he was over to see if I wanted to play a round at the country club.

"We're leaving," Barry said as he gestured to his house across the street. Over his shoulder I could see the garage was open, and his wife, Jill, was busy cramming stuff into the family minivan. "Jill wanted me to come over and see if you wanted to head out with us."

The offer didn't surprise me. For some reason, Jill was obsessed with me. I never knew why, and never bothered to ask, but I think it had something to do with the fact that I was a single executive and Barry was a mid-level accountant at the firm. I had financial freedom and my independence, and Jill was stuck at home with three kids and a never-ending pile of laundry. Jill was a fine woman, but she wasn't my type, and I never once reciprocated anything toward her, even when she came over one Sunday morning looking to borrow a cup of sugar and she was wearing nothing but a raincoat.

"Where are you going?" I asked.

Barry wiped the sweat from his brow onto his shirtsleeve. "Jill's folks have a place down in the mountains of Georgia, so we're headed there."

"Live off nuts and squirrels until things calm down?" I asked jokingly. I even chuckled after I said it.

"Something like that," Barry deadpanned.

"No. Thanks for the offer, but I've got a different destination in mind."

"Where?"

"Virginia," I blurted out before I thought about lying.

"What's in Virginia?" Barry asked.

"My great uncle used to live there. When he died, I inherited his farm," I said.

I watched Barry's eyes, and it looked like he was doing some accounting of his own. He opened his mouth and was about to say something when Jill appeared at his side.

"We'd better get going, honey," she said to Barry. "Hey Baker," she said as she finally acknowledged me.

"Jill," I said. "I hear you're headed for Georgia."

Before Jill could answer, Barry interrupted. "Baker's going to Virginia. We should go with him instead."

"What? Why?" Jill asked. I have to admit, those same questions hit my thoughts at the same time.

"He's got a farm there," Barry answered.

Jill looked at me dead in the eyes. I saw a flicker of anger in her eyes at first, then that quickly passed, and her countenance softened. I imagine she was trying to picture herself as a helpless farm girl caught in the barn and me as the hearty farmhand there to save her.

"It's less of a farm, and more of a homestead," I explained. "I haven't been there in years, and honestly have no idea what shape it's in." I hoped the truth would save me.

Jill looked at me, then back at Barry. From across the street, an infant began to cry.

"Barry, my parents are expecting us. It's time to go. Now." Jill gave me a last glance, then turned, ran across the road, and disappeared into the van.

"You sure you don't want to come with us?" Barry asked.

"Thanks for the offer, but no, man. You go take care of your family."

I extended my hand, and Barry shook it.

"Good luck," I said.

"Same to you. You're going to need it. I'm sure we'll see each other in a month or two."

"Probably," I agreed, even though I doubted it.

Barry nodded, hesitated for a second, then returned to his family. I watched as he closed all the van doors, then slipped into the driver's seat. A second later, the van backed out of the garage and into the street. Barry waited for the garage door to close, then he gave me a little wave and drove away.

I never saw Barry, Jill, or any of their three kids again.

CHAPTER TWO

Once Barry and family disappeared from view, I slipped back into my condo and returned to my bedroom where I spotted the leather suitcases laid out on the king-sized bed. Neatly folded in the case was the only thing I had packed so far: my favorite suit.

"What the hell are you thinking?" I said to no one. After all, an interview at this point seemed unlikely.

I returned the suit and oversized suitcase to the closet, and rummaged around until I found the only two pairs of jeans that I owned, both designers, of course. I threw those on the bed and added to the pile the three T-shirts I owned, along with a handful of socks and underwear. For footwear, I opted for my best running shoes. I put all the clothing into a duffel bag, then wandered to the bathroom and gathered a few sundries to take along as well. I zipped the duffel closed, then took a last look around the bedroom, wondering if I had forgotten anything. It turns out I did. I returned to the closet and pushed a few suits aside, revealing a false electrical breaker panel. I set the breakers for the garage, den, and hallway lights to the off position, then pulled on the double breaker for the kitchen. The entire breaker panel opened like a door, and from inside I retrieved my passport, several credit cards I used only for emergencies, and an envelope containing five thousand dollars in cash. I closed the safe door, set the breaker panel back in place, and reset all the switches.

I grabbed the duffel and headed downstairs. From the front closet, I grabbed my Yale sweatshirt, the sneakers I wore on the weekends, and my favorite windbreaker. The reason it was my favorite windbreaker was the secret pockets it contained. It contained about thirty pockets in various locations, all sized differently and able to hold everything from a ballpoint pen to a small laptop. Within the jacket I concealed my passport, credit cards, and cash, and slipped on the coat. I put on my shoes and stepped into the kitchen to find my car keys. The keys sat on the counter next to the fridge. I opened the fridge and looked inside. Because I wasn't much of a cook, I didn't have much in there except a few condiments and some takeout containers. Since I dare not guess how long I'd be gone, I removed everything from the fridge and freezer and dumped it all into a large garbage bag. I took the garbage and my duffel out to the garage and as I waited for the garage door to open, I locked the house.

Once I disposed of the trash, I threw the duffel into the backseat of my beloved Mustang convertible, started the car, and backed out of the garage. Instinctively, I reached forward to set the GPS for the journey, then sat back when I realized I didn't have the address for the farm. I wasn't sure it even had an address, other than a post office box in town. Luckily, I knew where it was though, and could get there by memory, and I certainly didn't need to map my way to the interstate. I drove slowly through my neighborhood, taking stock of what was going on around me. There seemed to be about a fifty-fifty split between people packing up and leaving and people hunkering down in their homes.

As I got farther away from the residential area, I noticed things got a little rougher as I got closer to the city. The roads appeared packed with people, and it seemed those people lost all desire to follow any traffic laws at all. Stoplights, yields, and speed limit signs looked more like suggestions. To their credit, most drivers still stayed on one side of the road, except in cases where they needed to drive around accidents or stalled cars.

I spotted a sign up ahead for a burger joint and my stomach rumbled since I hadn't eaten all day. Thoughts of a burger with extra onions and mustard danced through my head, but quickly exited when I noticed the burger place had burned to the ground, several spots still smoldering.

That's when I had my first revelation about the new world. Since I ate out most of the time, I took for granted not only food preparation but also where it came from. True, I now headed to the farm, but I knew nothing about farming, other than seeds grew into plants that a person might harvest and eat. As far as planting schedules, and how to tell an edible mushroom from a poisonous one? Clueless. And let's not even get into how to convert a cow into a hamburger. I was a city boy and had never once gone hunting or fishing or killed and cleaned anything. I did my hunting at the butcher's counter at the grocery store. Again, clueless. As I watched the smoke rise from the ruins of the restaurant, I wondered how long it would be before I starved to death.

Two blocks down from the restaurant, a mob of a couple dozen teenagers busted out storefront windows with baseball bats and tire irons. Not wanting to get in the middle of that, I made a right turn and decided to take a slight detour to the interstate.

I drove seven blocks before I saw the red, white, and blue shield that pointed the way to the interstate. I laughed as I turned the corner, knowing that the open road was only a quarter mile away, but that laughter stopped in short order as I almost ran into a Greyhound bus that was parked across all four lanes of traffic, blocking the way. In a panic, I slammed on the brakes, jerked to a stop, and threw the gears into reverse. Instinctively I checked the rear-view mirror, and in it I saw three old vans turn the corner and pull up until they almost touched my bumper, effectively trapping me in.

My heartbeat rose and my adrenaline spiked as I watched several men erupt from each van. Most seemed unarmed, but my concern was the ones who carried random items. Like the teens a few blocks down, the bat appeared to be the most popular weapon of choice, but there was a smattering of other things, including a samurai sword.

The leader of the pack approached my driver's side door, and I took a moment to double check the locks were engaged, even though I was stupid enough to put the Mustang's top and windows down. He didn't seem overly intimidating. He looked to be around thirty. His clothes looked clean, his hair looked neatly combed, and he had no visible scars or tattoos. Shit, give him a haircut and put him in a suit and he might have been my banker. His gang were about the same, all professional-looking men, not what the movies or the evening news made street gangs out to look like at all.

"Get out," he ordered.

"What do you want?" I stupidly asked.

He responded by reaching around to his back and producing the forty-five he had tucked into his belt.

"I want you to get out of the fucking car. Now."

"I…"

Before I finished the sentence, the banker stepped aside and, in his place, appeared by far the largest man I had ever seen. This guy stood at least six-six and had muscles on top of muscles. He looked like this was his first time out of the gym. Without a word, the muscle man reached into the car, wrapped his massive arms around me, and even though I weighed almost two hundred and thirty pounds, lifted me out of the car just as easy as lifting an egg out of a carton. He spun me around and dropped me on the ground where I not so gracefully stumbled and fell directly on my ass. Several of the men around me found that funny and laughed. How rude.

"Search him," the banker said. He wasn't much of a conversationalist, but he seemed to get his point across.

Two men approached, and each one grabbed one of my arms and pulled me to my feet. A third thug stepped forward, emptied all my pockets, and placed all the items on the hood of my car. I hoped he wasn't going to scratch the paint. The banker turned his attention to the stuff, and the first thing to disappear was my watch. The banker plucked it from the pile and tossed it to a man, who immediately added it to his wrist. I couldn't help but notice that he already had at least three watches on each arm. I figured he was obsessed with time. Next, the banker turned his attention to my wallet, an old leather wallet that had more sentimental value than actual worth. He pulled out the license, looked at it, then looked at me.

"Joshua Baker?"

"Yes." I responded.

"That's a pussy name. Your license expired two years ago. Is this your correct address?"

I thought for a second. Of course, the license had expired. Every license probably had. The one good thing about the collapse of the country was that no one bothered with the D.M.V. anymore. "No. I haven't lived there in three years."

The banker looked me in the eye, and I knew he knew I got caught in the lie.

"We'll see about that," he said as he tucked my license into his back pocket. At that moment, I knew I'd never be returning home again, and if I did, I'd find my place either destroyed or cleaned out.

From the wallet, the banker took a few receipts and tossed them into the wind, likewise the few business cards I had in there. He kept two credit cards and my twenty-seven dollars in cash, then tossed the wallet at me. Since the thugs still secured my arms, the wallet thumped against my chest, then fell into the street. The banker ignored the eighty cents in change, but grabbed the car keys, unlocked the door, and got comfortable in my seat.

"Hey!" I screamed. "That's my car!"

The banker flashed a smile at me. "Let's go," he said.

Most of the men scrambled into the vans, and the two that held me backed me away from my car until my foot caught the curb of the sidewalk and I tripped. They let me fall, ran back to the vans, and disappeared inside. With a screech of tires, all four vehicles reversed, then swung around. The blinking taillights were the last thing I ever saw of my beloved cherry red Mustang.

"Shit," I said as I sat on the sidewalk. My car was gone, but at least I was still alive. Since I had somewhat cooperated and hadn't put up a fight, the worst I had suffered was a pair of dirty jeans from falling into the street. My duffel with my clothes was still in the car, but I would replace those. The only bright side for me was since the gang seemed so interested in my car, they hadn't bothered to pat me down that well. True, I had lost the contents of my wallet, but I still wore my windbreaker, and in that I still had tucked away my cash, cards, and my passport. All seemed not lost. But I was.

Off in the distance, I heard a gunshot, and I knew that not all gangs on the streets would be as nice as the one that had just robbed me, so I took off on foot, eager to get off the street.

There was plenty of room for me to pass the bus on foot, and as I did, I peeked around the vehicle to see if anyone else was around. The street was empty, so I began to walk down the block. I ignored the on-ramp to the highway. Since I didn't have wheels, I didn't see the need to get there just yet. I wasn't going to walk all the way to Virginia. Still mad about losing my ride, I had hoofed it about three blocks when I heard another gunshot, and this one seemed to be louder and closer than the first. I looked around for a good place to hide, but I didn't see anywhere I could easily get into, and I didn't want to take the chance that the place I entered was already occupied. Warily, I kept walking along the street, then saw the sign for the pedestrian greenway. I followed the sign's arrow, and in another block, I found the trailhead of the city's latest addition to the miles of walking and biking trails around the town. Without hesitation, I started walking swiftly down the path. I doubted that a whole gang of people would take the trail, and if they did, I could easily step into the woods on either side of the path and hunker down until they passed.

Another gunshot pierced the quiet, but that one seemed farther away, so I slowed my pace and breathed easier, and fifty yards up the path, my luck finally changed for the better. An old ten-speed was leaning up against a tree. I approached the bike, pulled it onto the path, and gave it a once-over. Although the frame looked spotted with rust, the chain was intact, the tires were firm, and the brakes worked.

"Hello?" I called out. "Anyone there?"

I waited for a response, but there was none.

"Is this anyone's bike? Hello?"

I waited again, but again, no reply.

I threw one leg over the bike. The seat was a bit short for me, but I could easily fix that if I ever found a wrench. I kicked off, and with a wobbly start, headed down the path. I almost tipped over, then pedaled a few times to pick up speed and quickly righted myself. It turned out that riding a bike was just like riding a horse. Once you did it, you never forgot how, although I had never ridden a horse.

I followed the trail north at a comfortable pace and had covered at least two miles before the next trailhead appeared. I slowed down when the path reached the street and looked around. Again, I was alone. I debated continuing on the trail, but then decided that biking to Virginia was no more of an option than walking was, so I turned west onto the street and headed back to the general direction of town.

I pedaled for another mile, then saw a sign for Big Al's, and realized I knew exactly where I was. Big Al was a car dealer, well known for his crazy commercials that claimed he had acres and acres of cars, new and used, for the low, low price you could afford. With on-site financing. Couldn't beat a deal like that.

I followed the fence line of Big Al's lot, glancing at cars as I passed them. A quarter way down, I spotted a real beauty, the twin of my missing Mustang, but in royal blue, and I half considered it for a second before I rationalized I needed to go for something more functional and not quite so flashy. I kept biking until I came to the lot's wide-open gate, then slowly pedaled in toward the main building. Although Big Al had acres and acres of cars, he didn't have much in the way of an office. It looked like it was made of cinder blocks that were covered in a faded white paint. There was an attached car wash, and two bays for car repairs. I could tell someone had the same idea I had because, as I approached the main door, I could see that someone had busted out the plate-glass window. As I stepped through the doorway into a small reception area, the glass crunched under my feet.

"Hello? Anyone here?" I stupidly called out. Fortunately, I didn't get an answer.

Past the reception desk was a short hallway, and I entered that hallway to see what was beyond. There were four doors: one restroom, two offices, and a door I assumed led to the mechanic's bays. I picked the first office I came to and stepped into the ransacked mess. The chairs lay overturned, papers littered the floor, and the drawers from the desk and the two file cabinets sat piled on each other in the far corner of the room. I stepped out and entered the other office. That office was a bit bigger and had been gone through as well. Again, I found a mess, but this time I found a closet, and when I peeked inside, I discovered it wasn't a closet at all, but rather a large safe where I knew the business had stored the petty cash and car keys. Whoever had gotten there before me must have guessed the same, since there were random tools piled on the ground, including various sized hammers, a power drill, several screwdrivers, and a large crowbar. The safe was top-notch. Although there were a couple of dents on the door and the paint showed deep scratches in several places, it still looked firmly locked. Rather than try to open it myself, I walked out of the building and got back on the bike. I'd have to steal my new car from somewhere else.

I turned left out of the lot, still heading in a general northerly direction. Although I struggled with the few hills I encountered and my legs were aching, it felt good to be on a bike again. It had been way too long since I had gotten any decent exercise like that, and having the cushy position I did at the firm only helped to make me lazy and fat.

As I pedaled, I mentally made a list of things I needed, including a new backpack, clothing, and enough provisions to get me to Virginia. I was also still on the lookout for a vehicle, but each one I checked was either locked up tight, or obviously disabled, so I rode on.

After a few miles, I slowed to a stop, propped my foot on the curb, and looked behind me. Yep, I had seen it correctly, something people passed by every day without really noticing it, unless you needed to go there. The post office. I checked for traffic in both directions, then swung the bike around, crossed the street, and slipped into the vacant lot. Cautiously, I approached the front door, pulled on the handle, and it opened easily. I wheeled my bike inside and propped it up against a row of post office boxes and looked around. Except for a single piece of junk mail lying on the floor next to a garbage bin, the place was spotless.

I went to the inner door which led to the counter area and found it unlocked as well. Clearly, the postmaster hadn't bothered to batten down the hatches when they left, and why should they? The mail hadn't moved in months, and it's not like people were going to start bartering in postage stamps. It took me a bit of a struggle, but I managed to not-so-gracefully crawl over the counter into the back. I smiled at the pile of outgoing mail that would never reach its destination and made my way into the bowels of the station. There was a break room, a restroom, a large mail sorting area, and a door that led to the delivery dock. Next to that door was a small cabinet on the wall, and within that cabinet, hanging neatly on hooks, were a dozen keys.

I opened the dock door, glanced outside, and spotted a half dozen delivery vans parked nearby. I took all the keys from the cabinet and went outside to inspect the vans. Two I dismissed quickly because of flat tires, and one of them looked like it had been sitting there since the early 70s, but the other three looked fairly new. I crawled onto the seat of the closest one and tried keys until I found the one that fit. I attempted to turn it on, but the battery was dead. Disheartened, I moved on to the next mail truck, climbed into the cab, and found the key for that one. That truck fired right up. While I let the engine warm up, I looked in the back and determined that it would do quite nicely. There was certainly enough space in the back for storage for whatever I picked up, and I could easily stretch out on the floor for a nap if I got tired. I spent a few minutes dumping old mail out of the back of the truck, and once I cleaned it out, I headed back inside, retrieved my bike, and put it in the van. Then I slipped the van into Drive and headed toward the interstate. I felt good, like I had a plan. More importantly, I felt more secure. After all, who would stop me to steal a mail truck? At last, I was on my way to Virginia.

CHAPTER THREE

I was only an hour north of Charlotte when I realized that mail trucks didn't seem meant for long-distance travel. The seats didn't recline, there was no air conditioning, and the steering wheel was on the wrong side of the vehicle, which I admit took me some time to get used to, especially when going around corners. Since they built the truck like a box, the gas mileage wasn't all that great either. The highway sign I saw said that Elkin was only twenty miles up the road, so I made that my destination to stop for gas, find some food, and rest my already aching back. God, I missed my Mustang.

Once I pulled off the interstate and headed west on Highway 67, I realized Elkin didn't look so bad. There were people out and about, but unlike in the city, they didn't travel in packs, seemed nonthreatening, and generally just went about their business. Most of them waved, which brought a smile to my face as I waved back. Good old country hospitality. Not wanting to draw too much attention to myself, I found the local post office, and fortunately for me, it was a post office that had its own fuel pumps. I gassed up the mail truck, then left it locked and parked while I went for a walk to stretch my back muscles. A block up from the post office was a service station, and in front of that station was a man sitting on a bench sipping from a can of cola.

"Howdy," the man said as I approached.

"Good afternoon to you. Are you Red?" I asked. It was a reasonable assumption. The sign on the front of the building said 'Red's Garage', and the man on the bench was wearing mechanic's overalls, complete with a wrench sticking out of the front pocket. He also looked like a Red with his lanky build, gray hair, and stubby beard.

"Me, no. Red died in the early nineties. Ninety-two maybe? Cancer got him. I'm Donnie. I took over after Red died."

"Good to meet you," I said. "Maybe you can help me out. I'm looking for a gas can or two. I can pay."

"With what?" Donnie asked.

"Money. I can give you, let's say, twenty dollars a can?"

Donnie responded with a laugh, so hearty droplets of soda erupted from his mouth and splattered on the sidewalk. "Money? What the fuck would I do with money? Lemme guess, you're from the city, son?"

I nodded. "Charlotte."

"Figures," Donnie said as he wiped his chin. "See, you're from the city, thinking that money's the answer to everything. But it ain't. Not anymore. That way of life is done, at least for a little while until someone can right the ship again, but hell, how many years is that gonna take? The money was only good cuz the government backed the bills, but the government dent is gone. The toilet paper I have hidden in my barn is worth more than money now."

"Then why keep your shop open?" I asked.

"Barter, son. Barter's the new currency. Steve Johnson has a trolling motor he needs fixed. I fix his motor. He gives me eggs. I don't much like eggs, but Maisy Ross does, so I give her the eggs, and she gives me a pie. See how that works, son? We're back to the olden days. You need to start thinkin' like that. You need something to barter, whether it be a skill, service, knowledge, or goods. Of course, you might also be a scrounger or a thief, but I imagine those folks ain't going to last long. Got it?"

"Got it," I agreed. Donnie was right. It was a new world, which meant I needed to adjust my thinking. It also meant I was in deeper shit than I originally thought I was.

"Thanks for the words of advice," I said.

Donnie nodded, and I turned back toward the post office.

"You forgot the cans. There's four of them in the back of the bay. You're welcome to take the two that are empty."

I turned back around. "Are you sure? I have nothing to trade for them."

"Ain't you been listening, son? The world is different now. We haven't had a gasoline delivery in a while now, which means it's gonna start getting scarce. And even if you had a swimming pool full of it, it goes bad, you know."

I didn't know. And he knew that based on the stupid look I had on my face.

Donnie shook his head. "After about three months, the gas starts to go stale, especially if it ain't stored correctly. I'd say a year is about the limit. After that, I won't need the cans anymore, anyway. New world, new rules, son. Remember that."

Donnie took another drink of his cola, and I took advantage of the conversation break to retrieve the two gas cans.

"Thanks again," I said.

"You want some free advice to go with those cans?" Donnie asked. "You need to learn something."

Learn something? Had I heard that right? The words offended me. "I know plenty. I have a bachelor's in business and an MBA."

Donnie looked me dead in the eye. "Well, la-de-dah, Mr. MBA man. Did you learn anything gettin' that MBA that'll help you now? Like how to dig a well, or how to build a cookin' fire, or how to select a wild mushroom that won't kill you?"

He had me, and he knew it. "No," I capitulated.

"Well then," he said. "Good luck to you, Mr. MBA man."

I nodded, then returned to the post office, filled the gas cans, and stored them in the truck with my bike.

I fired up the truck and pulled out of the post office the opposite way from which I came, if only to avoid passing Donnie on Main Street, and a blue sign pointing toward the local library caught my eye. With a plan in mind, I turned the corner, drove three blocks, and pulled into the library's parking lot.

I locked the truck, and headed for the front door, wondering if it was open and staffed, but I assumed by the smashed-in glass that the days of the librarian had passed as well. Careful not to cut myself, I slipped in through the missing window and stepped into the library. I noticed someone had ransacked it, since the nearest book display was upended and there was a trail of random CDs and DVDs scattered from the door leading to where I assumed they had previously sat in the stacks. As I walked deeper into the depths, I noticed the initial mess was the only damage done, which made sense, since the only thing of value in a library is knowledge.

From behind the desk, I pulled an empty book cart and wheeled it with me to the non-fiction section. It would have been easier to find what I was looking for had there been a good old-fashioned paper card catalog, but I didn't have that option, so I resorted to browsing the shelves instead. I strolled up and down the aisles, selecting books at random and paging through them before I added them to the growing pile on the cart or setting it back on the shelf. After an hour of wandering around the non-fiction section, I moved over to the general fiction section and grabbed whatever they had by Grisham, Koontz, Cussler, and King, and added those to the pile.

The book cart was heavy as I pushed it through the library to the front door. Rather than transfer them by hand through the broken glass, I found the latch to unlock the door and wheeled the cart out to the truck. As I transferred the books to the truck, I kept a mental tally of what I had, including several books on gardening, a few cookbooks, small engine repair, home repair, first aid, herbal medicines, and a handful of field guides to help me identify anything from fowl and flora, to fauna and rocks. Between the non-fiction and fiction, I stacked just over fifty books into the truck with my bike and the gas cans.

Out of respect for the institution, I returned the book cart to where I found it and relocked the front door before slipping through the broken window.

As I strolled to the truck, I both heard and felt the growl emanating from my stomach. My last meal was breakfast before I left my house, and that seemed like months ago. I got in the truck and drove around the small town until I came across the local supermarket. Like the library, the store was unmanned, but unlike the library, the shelves were empty. Even so, I grabbed a shopping cart and pushed it up and down every aisle, and into the rear of the store, looking for anything I might find. In the end, my haul was a single can of wax beans, a box of kitchen matches, and a half-empty bottle of water that I drank down in four gulps.

In the general store next to the supermarket, my score was a little better. I scrounged up a sleeping bag, a small camp stove, and a hunting knife. It wasn't much, but I added my finds to the mail truck, then drove back to the garage.

Donnie was still sitting where I last saw him.

"Hey Donnie," I said, leaning out the window, "do you know where I can rustle up some food or water?"

Donnie stood and walked to me and leaned on the door. "Water's easy. There's a town square three blocks east of here with a tap that comes from the water tower. Still worked as of yesterday. Food, let's see, you remember Maisy Ross?"

"The pie lady?"

"Yeah, the pie lady. She's a widow, got a place just outside of town. Head toward the highway and take the first driveway on the right once you get past the 'Welcome to Elkin' sign. She's got a soft heart, so I imagine she'd trade you some food if you did a few chores around her place."

"Thanks," I said.

"Another lesson, for you, Mr. MBA man, wherever you're going, stay off the interstate. Take the opportunity of every town you go through to look for food. Stores, gas stations, places with vending machines, even houses if you know they're empty. You won't last long on an empty stomach."

"Thanks for the lesson." I saluted, then pulled away from the curb.

It turned out Donnie was right about Maisy Ross. She had a whole list of chores that needed to be done, and after I spent three hours working around her farm, she rewarded me with a sit-down meal and since the daylight was fading, an offer to sleep in her barn, which I took her up on.

The next morning, Maisy made me a small breakfast of one egg and two pieces of toast from homemade raisin bread, then surprised me with a half-dozen jars of canned vegetables and a jar of canned peaches. We said our goodbyes on the back porch, and I was back on the road.

Part of me wanted to ignore Donnie's advice and just get the rest of the drive over with since it would only be another three hours of road time, but I thought better of it, retrieved a road atlas I'd taken from the library, and plotted out a route along state roads instead.

My journey took almost a full day to get from Elkin to Pottsfield, Virginia, but the delay was worth it, as my bounty was growing exponentially. The first town I stopped in I found a moving supply store, so I wandered in and helped myself to several boxes and a few rolls of packing tape. With those, I packed away the books and organized everything else in the truck. At a gas station, I found an almost-full propane tank, and down the block I found seven five-gallon water jugs stacked nicely in a storeroom of a small gas station. Granted, the jugs were empty, but that was something I thought I could fix easily enough the next time I found a working tap, or a natural spring. I had paged through the water section of a survival guide to know enough that to be completely safe I'd have to either boil my water or find a filter or purification tablets somewhere, so I had already added those items to my growing list of things to watch out for.

I had just passed over the state line into Virginia when I entered a town so small I didn't even catch the name of it. There wasn't much to the town, and as the road changed from the highway number to Main Street, I didn't think my scrounging options would be too fruitful. When I got to the downtown area, which only comprised a single intersection with a four-way stop, I saw how little of a town it actually was. The north block contained a car dealership, and from the looks of the inventory, it hadn't sold a car in at least thirty-five years. The south block held an antique store with its plate-glass window busted out, and on the eastern corner stood a bank which had its front doors removed. What really caught my eye was the pharmacy that was sitting on the western side of the intersection. Unlike its neighboring buildings, the pharmacy didn't look like it had sustained any damage at all, and when I pulled up to the building, I realized why. Large metal grates protected the main door and window. I could tell someone had given their best effort to get in since there was a crowbar lying on the ground next to the door. There were several fresh scratches on the grate, but the defenses had held. I picked up the crowbar, got back into my truck, and pulled around to the alley of the building.

The pharmacy's rear was just as fortified as the front. The building was completely bricked in, except for a shipping dock door, which I could tell hadn't seemed breached, either. Looking around, the only possible entry point was a small second-story window positioned in the center of the building, about fifteen feet from the ground. It looked promising, so I positioned my truck beneath the window, then dug around in the back to retrieve the extension ladder I had found earlier in the day. I climbed up onto the roof of the truck and leaned the ladder against the building. The ladder ended about a foot below the window, but that was close enough. I grabbed the crowbar, then climbed the ladder.

When I reached the top, I peered through the window and saw that the room was a small office. Just beneath the window was a desk, with a single lamp and cluttered with paperwork, an uncomfortable looking wooden chair, and four five-drawer file cabinets. It looked promising.

I raised the crowbar to smash the window, but before I did, I simply pushed up on the frame. Not locked, the window slid open. Although the sash protested, I opened it wide enough to enter without having to break it. I scrambled down from the desk and left the room, where I found a set of rickety stairs that led to the bottom floor.

The stairs creaked and moaned as I descended. I could tell immediately no one had ransacked the pharmacy. Everything was in place on the shelves. There were no telltale signs of broken glass, no random piles of debris, nothing at all to indicate anyone else had been in the building. Until I wandered over to where they kept the good stuff. Upon first glance, when I approached the pharmacist's area, everything looked normal, but when I stepped in front of the door, I noticed the door was hanging only by the top hinge. Carefully, I pushed my way through the door and entered the restricted area, and once inside, I could tell that indeed a looter or two had been there before me. The shelves had little labels attached to where they housed the bottles of specific medicines, and the spots where the codeine, morphine, and anything with the suffix 'codone' were empty. In addition, there were other areas of empty shelves, but since I didn't recognize either the brand or generic names, I couldn't tell what had disappeared. Whoever had beaten me to the punch had left behind all the 'cillins', so I loaded up a bag with everything I recognized that could stave off an infection.

When I finished behind the counter, I strolled into the main area of the pharmacy, which turned out to be a cornucopia of goodies. Besides the drugs, nothing else looked touched. I grabbed a shopping cart from the corral near the front door, along with a handful of bags, and started my pilfering spree. First, I grabbed all the pain relievers, antacids, and cold and flu medicines that I could find. I filled up on every bottle of multivitamins that I could get my hands on. I stocked up on adhesive and regular bandages, and personal hygiene items such as toothpaste and mouthwash, and antibacterial and bar soaps, and toilet paper. Unfortunately, the pharmacy wasn't large enough to have a large number of foodstuffs, but it contained cases of bottled water, soda, and sports drinks, and I found a small snack aisle full of nuts, candy, and various flavors of beef jerky.

By the time I finished, I had four shopping carts filled with goodies. Now all I had to do was get out of the building without being seen.

I trudged back up the stairs and looked out the window. There wasn't a soul in sight, and I leaned my head out to listen for any sounds in the area. It was all quiet. I rushed back downstairs and found my way to the shipping dock area.

There was a button to open the shipping door, which I pushed, and the door rattled and squealed open so loudly I was certain a horde of people would appear at any moment. When the door stopped, I waited, ready to push the button to lower the door again, but after almost a full minute, no one came.

With great haste, I loaded everything into my truck, returned all the carts inside the building, then pushed the button to close the door. I slipped under the door and exited the pharmacy, returned to the truck, and soon I was on my way again.

CHAPTER FOUR

The clock in the car said it was but a few minutes after two in the afternoon when I turned off the county highway onto the rutted driveway that led to my new home. I wouldn't have even seen it but for the large 'Trespassers Will Be Violated - Or Worse' sign that someone nailed to a large oak tree right next to the road. Like most signs in this part of the county, it stood at a slight slant and pitted with bullet holes from being used as target practice.

Going no more than five miles an hour, lest I break an axle in the bevy of potholes along the trail, I drove about a quarter mile before the road split, and I had my choice of going left or right. Although I hadn't been to the property in many years, I remembered that turning left would take me down the mountain and into the valley where my new property sat. Although I felt tired and guessed I had a fair amount of work ahead of me, I took the fork to the right instead, which led farther up the mountain.

At one point the road narrowed to nothing more than a track, and the trees closed in to where the branch limbs on either side scrapped against the truck, but I kept going until the road widened and a small log house came into view. Now, when I say it was a log house, I meant a real log house, not one of those faux log houses that seemed all the rage back in the early nineties. They had probably laid the original logs of this old house back when James Buchanan served as president. I could tell the house had gone through many renovations since then, first adding on to the original footprint, then adding a second story. Sure, I had never been inside, but I guessed a couple of the add-ons would have been a modern kitchen and indoor plumbing. I could tell by the lines overhead that he had electricity, and an enormous satellite dish pointed to the heavens stood sentinel on the roof.

As I parked the truck and slid out of the driver's seat, I wondered if anyone was home, but that question got answered when I heard a screen door screech open, and slam closed. A second later I heard barking dogs running toward me, and I hoped they didn't think I was a real mailman. When the dogs ran to within two feet of me, they both stopped, stood guard, and growled. I'm not really a dog person, so I didn't know what breed they were, but they looked like mutts to me. The one that concerned me the most looked like it had some pit bull in him, just based on the shape of the head. That one had dark brown fur and looked like he wanted to eat my face for lunch. The other dog looked a little friendlier, had a coat of long, golden fur, and could have been a collie or a shepherd mix, but I couldn't tell for sure.

I put my hand on the door handle, ready to make my retreat, when a man called out.

"Who are you there?"

I got so focused on the dogs that I never noticed the homeowner standing just off the porch with a shotgun pointed in my direction. I raised my hands in the air on instinct.

"Pops, is that you?" I yelled back.

"I know who I am. Tell me who you are," came the terse reply.

"Pops, I'm Albert's nephew. When he died, I inherited the property. We're neighbors now. I've come to live here."

Pops took a few strides toward me but didn't lower the gun. Considering we stood on a mountaintop in rural Virginia, I half expected the man to be wearing overalls with one strap undone and no shoes, to go with a long white beard and a straw hat, but that stereotype got blown away by the person before me who wore a pair of faded jeans, what looked to be homemade moccasins, and a Bruce Springsteen T-shirt. He had a white beard, but he wore it neatly trimmed, and he wore no hat.

He took another step closer and stared at my face. Finally, he lowered the gun.

"You look like your mama," he acknowledged.

"So, I've been told."

I stretched out my hand to shake, but the dogs barked at the motion.

"Frank, Dino. Down. Go," Pops said to the beasts. They stopped barking, turned, and trotted back to the shadows of the front porch.

Pops accepted my hand, and we shook. He led me to the porch, and we sat in mismatched rocking chairs.

"Shame about Al. He was a good man. We'd get together a couple of times a week. Throw some steaks on the grill, play cribbage. I miss him."

I had little to say, since I hadn't seen my uncle for at least a decade.

"He said you worked as an attorney down in Atlanta, right?"

"Close. H.R. manager from Charlotte," I answered.

"Why'd you decide to come up here?" Pops asked.

"After the collapse of everything, the city became too dangerous. Limited resources, except guns and ammo, those seem to be in good supply. It got to a point where you didn't know if the person you passed on the street was going to say hello or stab you in the neck to steal your shoes. I thought coming here would be a better idea."

"Probably the best idea you ever had. You can easily live off the land here as long as you learn how to work it. Ever grow crops? Hunt?"

I shook my head. "No. Neither. I can learn, though."

"Yep, you can. I've been keeping up Al's small garden since he passed. Hope you don't mind. I'd be willing to sharecrop it with you, since technically it's yours."

"No problem," I said. "I appreciate you keeping it going. Anything else I should know about the property?"

Pops thought for a moment, and as he did, the black dog, Frank, laid down next to his chair. Pops leaned over and scratched Frank's head, and Frank let out a canine sigh and closed his eyes.

"Biggest benefit to this land is we're far enough off the main road to not be conspicuous. Sure, there are lots of people who know I'm out here, but your average roving band of murderers and thieves wouldn't think twice about coming up the driveway. To be less noticeable, I've been thinking about taking down that old sign. Maybe obscuring the road up here somehow."

"I'm glad that sign was there. Wouldn't have found the place otherwise."

"Well, I'll leave it up then until you become accustomed to the area. Once you're comfortable coming and going, I'll remove it. Other than the small garden, you've got good water and enough acreage to plant more crops if you want. It's your place. I'd recommend just wandering around the property and deciding how much you want to do with it."

"What about property lines? What other neighbors do I have around here?"

"Just me. Your spread and mine are the only ones out here. To the south, east, and west, the property ends at the highway and state roads. On your side to the north, there's what used to be state game land, and that's marked pretty good, so you'll spot it when you venture over there. The line between yours and mine is somewhere up the side of this mountain, but neither Al nor I ever had the desire to map out exactly where it was. It's not like we were gonna build a fence. Share and share alike is what we did. When I kept horses, he let me stable them in his barn and graze on his land. He'd come up here to hunt. We found that working together benefited both of us, and I'd appreciate it if you and me might make that same arrangement."

I didn't even have to think about it. "Sure thing," I said.

Pops squinted at me, even though there was no sun in his eyes. "When was the last time you visited here?"

That was a hard question to answer. I had to dig through the memories of my mind like I panned for gold.

"I don't know. Fifteen, twenty years perhaps. Why?"

Pops smiled, then laughed. "Since you were here last, your uncle started a… collection of some things."

That made me curious. "What things?"

Pops winked at me. "I don't want to spoil the surprise."

I stayed with Pops for another hour. He gave me a tour of the inside of his place, which included electricity and a bathroom, complete with a jacuzzi tub and a walk-in shower. The satellite on the roof was connected to the large screen television, complete with a Blu-ray player and a sound system setup. Along one wall of his main living room were shelves overflowing with books, movies, and vinyl records. The kitchen was upscale and full of cooking gadgets, and the bedroom held a king-size bed and furniture that looked like he made them from the trees on his land.

He introduced me formally to the dogs, Frank and Dino, named after Sinatra and Martin respectively, and had me feed them treats and play with them so they'd recognize me as a friend and not a potential snack. Then, eager to settle into my place, I said goodbye and drove the truck down the mountain to my new home. There was a spot along the driveway where it rose over a small hill, and when I crested it, I hit the brake and looked over my kingdom. What I saw both took my breath away and sent a shudder down my spine.

The valley below me looked like a postcard. Beyond the buildings, there spread a wide-open field, and I could tell that the field had held food crops at one time. I noticed whatever my uncle planted in there had gone wild and was now interspersed with tall grasses. A section of land stood surrounded by wood fencing that blocked off the pasture Pops had mentioned. On the far side of the valley floor there stood a tree line, straight as an arrow, where I assumed the state land started, and twenty yards before the trees I spotted a stream that fed into a pond. It looked like an excellent place to put down both literal and figurative roots.

Then I refocused on the buildings. There was the main house that looked to be the same size as the one Pops lived in. There was an enormous barn, which I also expected to see, since Pops talked about keeping his horses there. What I didn't expect to see was off to the left side of the property, perhaps two hundred yards from the house, was a veritable junkyard. Visible to me sat not one, but two mobile homes that looked like they came right out of the seventies. Parked next to one of them was a full-sized RV. I assume it started out as white, but from a distance, it appeared to wear a color palette of dirty light brown and mossy light green. Although I couldn't see behind the mobile homes, I did see the remains of a rusted car between the buildings, so I assumed there was at least one old car back there. I took a deep breath, then drove down to the house.

I parked in the driveway close to the house and walked to the front door. When I got to the porch, I unzipped secret pockets until I found the keys to the house. The door had three locks on it. The lock on the door handle, and two deadbolts. I had six keys in my hand, so it took some trial and error until I unlocked the door and swung it open.

As soon as I opened the door, that familiar musty smell of a house shut up for too long rushed out the door like it was a living thing trapped for too long. I stepped in the door and looked around but couldn't see much since the only light was what streamed in through the door behind me. To my right, I found a light switch, and I flipped it on. The ceiling light came on, and I was immediately sorry I had come in. I shook my head as the first things I saw were the piles that took up every inch of space in the room, except for a narrow path that led to other rooms of the house. The piles seemed to be mostly paper items, which accounted for the smell in the room. I spotted stacks of newspapers and magazines, but most of the stacks were books. There had to be hundreds, if not thousands, of books stacked tall not only on the floor, but on every inch of furniture. It surprised me that the room hadn't caught fire at some point and burned down the house.

The next thing I noticed was the dust covering everything. Everything. The books, curtains, what furniture I could see, the walls. The third thing of note was the impressive array of spiderwebs that hung around the ceiling. They dripped from the ceiling light and covered most of the area between the tops of the walls and the ceiling like bunting ready for a parade. I knew I had some work ahead of me, and although I hadn't lifted a finger to do anything, I felt already exhausted. Daunted, I didn't want to explore any further, but I pushed on anyway. I picked a path at random and followed it into the next room, which I discovered when I turned on the light, to be a bedroom. Once again, the sight shocked me.

Based on the living room, I expected this room to be a mess as well, but to my surprise, it wasn't. Other than the dust and spiderwebs, the room was moderately clean. The furniture looked cheap, but functional. The bed stood made complete with a comforter that looked like a generational heirloom. It appeared the room was a corner room, and since I had space to move around, I opened the curtains and the windows to let some fresh air in. Satisfied, I went back to the living room, and took the next trail between the books, which led me to another bedroom, a small bathroom, and once I got to the back of the house, the kitchen. To my relief, the only room with a big mess remained the living room, and I felt more positive energy flow through the house as I opened windows to let in the sunlight.

Someone, I suspect Pops, had cleaned out the refrigerator, as well as all the food from the cabinets, so I didn't see any bug or mouse droppings anywhere in the kitchen.

Overall, the house wasn't nearly as impressive as Pops' house, but it looked comfortable and good enough for me. It would take a little work to get it scrubbed down and cleaned up, especially in the living room. I thought a change of drapery and a fresh coat of paint everywhere would do wonders.

I unlocked the back door and stepped outside into the yard. The barn sat off to my right, and right in front of me, perhaps a hundred yards away, was the garden. The way Pops referred to it as a garden had me thinking about a few tomato plants and perhaps some cucumbers. Boy, I had that assumption wrong.

The garden looked about half the size of a football field. Sure, there were tomato plants and cucumbers, but as I walked around the perimeter, I spotted peas, beans, several types of squash, and small patches of sunflowers and sweet corn. There was a large patch where it appeared nothing looked planted, but I assumed there were maybe potatoes or sweet potatoes planted there. It was, in a word, impressive, and I gave a silent thanks to Pops since there was not only more than enough food here for the both of us but also plenty left over to barter or can, once I learned how to can.

I worked my way over to the barn and when I got there, I discovered padlocks secured the doors. I hoped the keys were in the house somewhere, but if not, I was sure I could use my trusty new crowbar to open the doors.

From the barn, I wandered to the mobile homes. Unlike the barn, the doors of both were unlocked. Since they were closed up, both needed fresh air, so I opened every door and window. One of the mobile homes looked like someone had lived in it at one point. There were personal belongings, photographs, clothing strewn about, and food in the kitchen. Although I begged myself not to, out of some morbid curiosity, I opened the fridge door. I expected an array of spoiled food and crusted bottles of condiments, but instead I found it filled with nothing but canned beer. I picked out a can. It was warm, so I placed it back and closed the door.

The other mobile home I entered was empty, other than the dust and ever-present spiderwebs. The mattress in the bedroom had a plastic cover wrapping, so I decided to sleep there until I had the main house cleaned.

I checked out the RV next. Before I ever got there, I could tell it was dead since the hood was open and there appeared to be parts removed from the engine. A quick walk around showed the tires were either missing or flat. I didn't bother going in.

Behind the mobile homes was what I expected in that there were a dozen junked cars of various ages, makes, and models scattered around the area. I never understood why people had old cars around their property, let alone the old fire engine that stood like a silent sentinel among them. But then I realized I was now one of those people, and I guess since the junkyard was probably closed, the pile would stay until I either towed them away myself or nature rusted them away to nothing.

I returned to the kitchen in the main house and underneath the sink I found what I was looking for, which was a bottle of all-purpose cleaner. In the hall closet, I found a bucket and some old towels. It surprised me when I opened the faucet of the bathtub and water streamed out, although in a dark shade of rust. I let the water run for a while, and although it never warmed, it ran clear after a few minutes. Once it did, I splashed some cleaner into the bucket and added water before I turned off the tap. I returned to the mobile home, entered the bedroom, and scrubbed everything down: furniture, walls, baseboards, and finally the linoleum floor. There was no water in the mobile home, so I had to make a few trips back to the main house before all my cleaning was complete. By the time I finished, the mobile home was still musty, but there was now an overtone of fresh lemon to it.

Once the cleaning was done, I moved a few of my possessions from the mail truck into the bedroom with me. My sleeping bag, a pillow, a few bottles of water, and enough food for the night. Fortunately, although the water was out, the electricity worked, so after I ate a meager dinner of canned vegetables and beef jerky, I sketched out a list of things to do around the property to get settled. As I reviewed the list, the lights flickered, went out for about ten seconds, then came back on.

At the top of the list, I added a new word in big block letters, then drew a box around the word. That word was 'power'.

CHAPTER FIVE

I slept in the next morning, not surprising considering everything I had been through the previous days. I woke to find my muscles were stiff. Once I rose, I dressed and stepped outside. I urinated in the yard, then stretched and jogged for a few minutes until my body loosened up.

Once I felt more like myself, I got in the truck and drove up the mountain, hoping to see if Pops was around. As I turned off the engine, I spotted him coming out of the ancient outhouse that bordered the clearing with the woods.

"How was your first night at the homestead?" he asked with a grin on his face.

"Better than I thought it would be," I confessed. "Was it you who cleaned out the kitchen?"

Pops nodded. "Couldn't let the food go to waste, could I? Did you like the library?"

I shook my head. "Not really what I was expecting when I opened the door."

Pops laughed. "I'll bet not. I have no clue why he started collecting all those books. It's like in his last year or two, he got obsessed with collecting them. He'd go to estate sales and library sales all over the county. Of course, the bookstores and Internet sites didn't help much. What're you going to do with them?"

"Probably move them out to the barn or into one of the mobile homes. I certainly don't want them in the house. Hey, speaking of the barn, do you know anything about the locks on the door?"

"No, but you'll probably find the key in the house somewhere. Once I got rid of the horses, Al started storing all his favorite toys in there."

"One last thing," I started, "what can you tell me about the water, sewer, and power down there?"

"Why? Having problems?"

"Well, I have water in the main house, unheated, and the power flickered on me last night in the mobile home."

"Water shouldn't be a problem. It comes out of a deep spring on the edge of your property. We're on the same pump. Since I'm still here, I've been maintaining the system to make sure the taps still work when I turn them on. Not sure what's wrong with your water heater, but I'm sure we can figure it out. For sewer, we have buried septic systems, probably last pumped out about five years ago. Since Al's been gone for four of those, you probably have a lot of space left in that tank, which is good, since I doubt the honey wagon will come around anytime soon. Power's another thing. Follow me."

Pops rose from his chair, and I followed him around to the back of the house, where he pointed to the roof. "See there?"

"Solar?" I guessed.

"Yep. I put those up before the world ended, since it's not uncommon for me to have power outages up here even in the best of times. So, I get most of my power from the sun now, even though I'm still hooked up to the grid. I don't know how long the grid will last though, since it'll only take one blown transformer or some downed lines to cut us off."

"You recommend I put up solar?"

"I would if I were you. I'd look into wind power too, since you get a lot of that down through the valley."

"Pops, I don't know anything about wind or solar," I admitted.

"Unless you want to live by candlelight and fire, I suggest you learn right quick," Pops said as he walked away.

I thought about Pops' advice as I drove back to the house. After I parked the truck, I opened the back door and sorted through all the boxes of books I had. Out of every book I thought to grab, alternative energy sources weren't one of them. I decided to take a trip into town to bridge that gap. Before I left, I unloaded the truck and put everything into the mobile home since I didn't want anyone to discover a full truck of goodies and steal it, especially since I worked so hard to steal all the stuff in the first place. I wished I had a key to the mobile home, but I didn't, so the best I could do was hope I wouldn't have any visitors before I returned.

Rather than go to the nearest town, which wasn't much of anything, I drove another twenty miles farther to what they classified as an actual city. Just past the city limits, I spotted a post office with its own gas supply, so I took the liberty to top off my tanks. I found a few empty gas cans, so I filled those as well and put them in the truck. After the post office, I stopped at a looted gas station and found a city map, and after a few minutes of study, I was on my way to the only library. Once there, I broke in, and within a half hour I left with a stack of books on the principles of electricity, how-to guides on converting to alternative energy sources, and a few other books on the topic. To my relief, I also found a planting guide specific to my region, so I pilfered that as well.

I drove back to the post office and parked in the lot right next to another truck so as not to arouse suspicion, and then I paged through the books, concentrating on the solar energy. I'll admit that some of it was way over my head, but I got the basics down enough to know I needed roof panels, battery banks, and a bunch of cabling. Now I just needed to figure out where to get it. The obvious place was a home improvement store, and it didn't take long driving in circles until I found one, well, two, actually, since they stood only a block from each other. The first store I entered with hope and grabbed a cart for my shopping pleasure. It took a bit to find the solar display, but I found it eventually. There was nothing more than descriptions of the various options with a sign to contact a salesperson to grab one for you. This implied to me that rather than being stocked on the shelf, they got stored in the back. I noted the brand, model number, and SKU and pushed the cart into the warehouse section of the store. I could tell scavengers had picked it through since cardboard boxes were open, merchandise was off the shelves, and the area was in disarray, but I picked my way through the refuse, anyway.

Luckily, I found what I was looking for at the far end of the building. There was only one whole-home system spread among several boxes, and I gathered them together. Thanks to my good luck, I snagged a couple of spare batteries as well. Since I had no desire to make at least three trips out the front of the store, I propped open the back door, then pulled my truck around to the receiving dock. I loaded up the truck, then headed back inside for another look around. Then I hit pay dirt when I found a stack of four solar generators hidden away under a tarp, so I hauled those to the truck too, including the tarp, which I used to cover everything in the truck. I returned to the store for a third time, and this time I pushed my cart up and down the aisles scrounging anything I thought might be helpful. Most of the tool sets had disappeared, but I found a screwdriver set, a ball peen hammer, a level, and an ax. I also scored a few boxes of nails and a single box of deck screws. In the cleaning aisle, I found my biggest score since it was almost fully stocked. Apparently, when the world collapsed, society decided there was no longer a need for toilet or window cleaner, which was fine by me. I grabbed three 32-gallon trash cans with lids and attached dollies in the same aisle, so I filled each of them full of various cleaning chemicals, rags, brooms, mops, and trash bags. The wood aisle stood empty, but if I had a need for chain or PVC, those had been virtually untouched. I also had my choice of toilets and light fixtures, but the appliances were all gone. It pleased me to find the paint department shelves stocked with cans of paint, and I made a mental note to remember that after I decided which color palette to go with back at the house.

After loading the truck, I took the time to explore the city for a while, mainly looking to discover who was out and about and if I had any chance to find food. I spotted a few dozen people as I drove around, mostly walking in twos or threes, but there were several folks brave enough to venture out alone. I didn't see many cars on the road, in all, I counted five. Two were muscle cars driven by teenagers racing through the streets, along with one van, one food truck I thought about following, and the last an ancient red pickup truck with a bed loaded down with wood and metal scrap. For the most part, people ignored me and proceeded about their business, but as I slowed to account for a woman crossing the street, she drew a long gun from underneath her coat and pointed it at me. I swerved and sped up. Behind me, I heard the report of the rifle, followed by the sound of something striking the back of my truck. She actually shot at me, and that removed any sense of adventure I had for the day, so I turned the next corner and followed the road east toward home.

Once back in my neck of the woods, I stopped at Pops' place and showed him what I had collected. I was relieved when he said what I had found would be good for a start, and he agreed to help me set things up the next day if the rain held off. I scratched Frank and Dino behind the ears and headed back to my place, where I parked the truck near the back door and stepped into the kitchen.

Much to my dismay, no cleaning crew came in while I was gone, so the kitchen looked just as dusty and gross as when I left it, except for the addition of my footprints traversing the floor. I decided that was as good of a place as any to start, so I rummaged around in the truck until I found enough cleaning supplies to get the job going. I spent the next few hours removing things from the drawers and cabinets, wiping the cabinets down, washing whatever I had removed, and replacing all the items to where I found them. Usually, the refrigerator was the worst part of cleaning a kitchen, but since it was empty and unplugged, it turned out to be a breeze. Even the oven wasn't that dirty, since my uncle had lined the bottom with aluminum foil. I stripped the old foil out, wiped it down, and it was good to go. I cleaned the small, two-person table, the mismatched chairs, and the pantry shelves. Weary, and with my muscles aching, I mopped the floor. When I finished, I dumped the mop bucket out behind the house and dragged my tired bones back to my bed. I had barely enough energy to scrape up a few things for dinner, and then I fell asleep.

The next morning, I woke to the sound of rain pattering on the ceiling. I rose, went to the door, and glanced outside. At first, I didn't think the rain was falling too hard, but I looked to the west and saw the clouds turn from light to dark gray, then almost to solid black. I saw a flash of lightning and heard a rumble of thunder, and knew the worst was yet to come. I had a quick bite, put on a pair of sweatpants and a T-shirt, and ran between raindrops to the main house. Since I knew the day would be a literal wash, I got determined to continue my cleaning.

I started the day in the home's only bathroom. It wasn't nearly as grandiose as the one Pops had, but it was good enough for just me. The sink vanity had one large door, and three doors down the side, and I started there. Normally I would toss out anything expired, but since these weren't normal times, I kept anything I thought I might use. I threw out Uncle Al's used toothbrush and razor, but I found unopened spares of each that I put aside. I saved open bottles of shampoo and conditioner, and a half-full tube of toothpaste. Then I sorted through random bottles of medicines and elixirs and ended up keeping most of it. Everything got a good scrub down, and the sparkle I saw when I finally finished pleased me.

From there, I moved into the master bedroom. Before I started the cleaning, I went through the bureau drawers to scan for any clothing I could salvage. I stood five-nine, and weighed in at a plump two-twenty, and my uncle was a good four inches shorter and at least fifty pounds lighter. In the end, only saved a dozen pairs of athletic socks, and the rest of the clothing I stacked over the books in the living room. Once I washed out the bureau, I stripped the bed and threw the blankets and sheets into the living room with the clothing. The mattress felt firm and fairly new, and like the mattress in the mobile home, enclosed within a mattress cover. After I wiped down the head and foot boards of the bed, I sat on the side of the bed and opened the top drawer of the nightstand. Within the drawer were a collection of random pens, old receipts and other slips of paper, scattered coins, and a porcelain coffee mug that contained several keys to vehicles, padlocks, and houses. I removed the mug and carted it out to the kitchen. I hoped one of the keys would open the barn.

Back in the bedroom, I opened the bottom drawer of the nightstand, which contained only three items. The first item I picked up was a leather-bound Bible. I didn't think my uncle was a religious man, and neither was I. I opened the book and just inside the front cover showed a listing of my family tree. I didn't recognize any names until I reached the last line and spotted the names of my great-grandparents. There were several folded sheets of paper within the Bible, and as I opened and read them, I realized I had a nice accounting of my family history going back almost four hundred years. It fascinated me and it sadly dawned on me I was the last person in that familial line. I vowed that when I found the time, I would fill in any recent names and dates, if only for posterity.

I turned my attention back to the drawer and pulled out the other two items. One was a handgun, the other a box of bullets. I guessed the caliber of the gun was a 9mm, but that was based simply on the writing on the box. I opened the box and saw a few bullets missing, and I assumed they were in the gun. Since I had never handled a handgun before, I didn't know if the safety was on, or if I was going to shoot myself, so I set it carefully back in the drawer, returned the bullets and Bible, and made a mental note to ask Pops about it.

The closet was a small one, and within it I found an old brown suit, several pairs of shoes that were at least two sizes too small for me, and a variety of jeans, cardigan sweaters, two sweatshirts, and three dress shirts. I moved all the clothing to the living room and washed down the closet. Next, I stood on the bed to remove the dusty curtains, then I cleared away all the cobwebs, wiped the baseboards, and swept and mopped the floor. Another room down.

I took a quick break, then cleaned the front bedroom. That only left the living room. I pulled one of the kitchen chairs to the living room's threshold, sat down, and took a deep breath as I stared at the mess. I pondered for a while, then figured I'd haul everything out to the mobile home I wouldn't use.

A rumble of thunder pealed through the house, and I remembered the storm outside. It had rained all day, but after I got into the groove of cleaning and sorting, the thunder and rain became background noise, barely noticeable. I stood, walked to the front door, and peered out. It was still coming down pretty good, although the sky had lightened a great deal since the ominous storm clouds in the morning. The worst of it would be over soon, but I didn't want to make a hundred trips back and forth between the house and the home in the rain, regardless of how heavy it fell. Instead, I gathered up as many empty boxes as I could find and packed up the books, magazines, newspapers, and clothing. When I finished, I had a dozen boxes stacked neatly along one wall, but I hadn't touched more than ten percent of the items in the room. The rain had tapered off to a drizzle, and my desire to move the boxes had washed away, so I decided to check if any of the keys I found would unlock the barn. In the kitchen, I dumped the mug of keys onto the counter and sorted through them. I pushed aside the car and house keys and picked up any keys that would fit a padlock, then jogged through the wet grass to the barn. I tripped the shackle with the third key, removed the lock, and pushed the door open.

To be honest, when I opened the door, I expected nothing but empty horse stalls with dirt floors, a hayloft complete with a pitchfork, and a saddle draped over a gate. When I flipped on the lights, bright light flooded the barn and lit up a space that blew my expectations away. The barn floor was concrete, not dirt. On the left side of the barn sat a dark blue pickup truck, two ATVs, trailers for each ATV, and a small backhoe. On the right side stood a tractor and several machines I didn't recognize, but I assumed were farm related. I saw a set of stairs and climbed up to the loft. Rather than hay, the loft contained a workshop with a tool bench that spanned an entire wall with pegboards on the wall that contained every manner of tool I could imagine, including several tools I dare not guess the purpose of. There were various machines for metalwork, including a drill press and grinders, and a bench saw among the items. There were several shelving units, and they were all stocked with all manner of things. Screws, nails, nuts, bolts, wire, do-dads, and knickknacks. I'm sure all the items had a purpose, but since my general knowledge was pretty much limited to lefty-loosey, righty-tighty, I figured I had a lot to learn about farm life. One shelf that provided some hope stood filled with owners and technical manuals, including ones for the ATVs and the various farming machines. I always figured that if I had a book, I could figure it out.

The next six weeks passed quickly, as there was so much to do. I finished cleaning out the main house and moved into it. That, and painting every room, were accomplishments I did solely by myself. Everything else Pops helped with. Together, we tended the garden, and he taught me the basics of canning to preserve the vegetables. He taught me about guns, and how to shoot the 9mm from the nightstand, as well as the hunting rifle I found behind a bookshelf when I cleaned out the living room. We added solar power to the main house and the barn, which turned out to be not as hard as I thought it would be. In fact, the biggest headache was scavenging the solar panels and other parts, but eventually we got it done.

Pops showed me how to maintain the water pump, and how to use a still to purify the river water. He taught me how to use the machinery in the barn, and we got started on a project to convert a diesel pickup truck to run on vegetable oil. Gasoline was getting harder to find, but there were hundreds of places within a forty-mile radius where I could get my hands on vegetable oil. Pops also took me into town, introduced me around, and taught me who I could barter with, and who would cheat me. Left on my own, I would have died within the first three weeks, but thanks to Pops, I knew I was going to make it. I had my home and plenty of resources as I settled in. I felt at peace and knew my future looked bright.

CHAPTER SIX

The sky was still dark when I woke, which was unusual for me since I naturally woke at dawn every day. At least, unless I spent the evening at Pops' place imbibing in his homemade hooch. The mornings after those events, I always slept in. I lay in the dark and listened, because something woke me from the dream I was having. Struggling, I propped myself up on one elbow and listened. I heard it again. It sounded like a smoke detector battery was going dead, or perhaps the microwave was beeping, but I realized neither was the case since the microwave didn't work and I didn't own any smoke detectors.

I caught the sound again, threw my blankets aside and got out of bed and plodded into the kitchen, rubbing the sleep from my eyes as I did. The beep sounded again, and I finally realized where it was coming from. I had a satellite phone on the counter, right under the kitchen window where it received a solar charge every day from the afternoon sun. I had forgotten all about the phone until I found the thing when I cleaned out all the secret pockets in my windbreaker. It beeped again. I had never gotten a call on it before because only one person had the number, and I guessed that person would only call me in an emergency.

I picked up the phone. Its presence seemed strange in my hand considering that in the old days, people didn't think twice about picking up their phone thirty times a day to text someone, or snap a photo, or check the net. It became an extension of their arm, and they did everything with it except make a phone call. It beeped again and vibrated slightly.

I hit the green button and placed the unit to my ear. There was a click, and I spoke.

"Hello?"

"Baker? Can you hear me?"

"Kayla? Hello? Are you okay?" I realized that was a stupid question the second I asked. She wouldn't be calling otherwise. I perceived a sniff.

"Jon died yesterday."

"I'm so sorry. What happened?" I asked.

"His diabetes got him. I tried to find insulin. I looked everywhere for drugs. Even searched almost as far as Dallas. I tried to trade, but no one had any. So many times, I tried and failed."

I overheard her break into tears, although she pulled away from the phone to hide it. I felt based on the type of person she was that she did everything she could do, but in these times, more often than not, the best wasn't good enough.

"You're not to blame," I said. What else could I say?

I listened to her cry for several minutes, and eventually she calmed.

"I don't know what to do," she whispered.

"Are you still in Oklahoma?" I asked.

"No. We moved back to Texas about a year ago to be closer to my parents."

"How are they?"

"Gone. They got trapped in a food riot a few months ago and didn't make it out."

"My god. I'm so sorry, Kayla." I didn't know where to go from there, and I guessed my condolences offered little in terms of comfort.

"With Jon gone, I'm all alone now."

She paused, as if getting up the courage to say something else, and I suspected what it was before she said a word.

"Do you remember the promise you made to me?"

And there the penny dropped. The promise. I remembered the promise very well. I made that promise years ago, long before the world turned to shit. That was back in the days of sit-down restaurants, and football on Monday nights, and Internet shopping. Long before Kayla's husband and my move to Charlotte. It felt like a million years since I made that promise.

"Yes. I promised to help you if ever you needed me to. Whatever. Whenever. Wherever."

"You called them the three W's."

That part I had forgotten, but it sounded like something I'd say.

"Baker? You there?" she asked.

"Yes, still here. Just thinking."

"I recognize I'm asking a lot, but you're my last hope. Baker, I know no one here, and I don't trust anyone enough to try to meet new people."

"I agree. You shouldn't do that. It's too dangerous to be on your own. You were right to call me."

"So, you'll come?"

"I will," I said immediately.

"Where are you?" I asked.

"At my parents' place. In Rice."

"I've never heard of it. Where is that in relation to the nearest large city?"

"Rice is about forty miles south of Dallas on I-45. Your average small Texas town."

"Tell me about your parent's place. Do they live on a ranch?"

"No. They only have a small house off a few blocks from the interstate."

"Okay. What about the area? Any farms? Good land? Water?"

"We get a fair amount of rain every year. Most of the farms around here are ranches that raise cattle or chickens. The grass grows, so the soil must be good, right?"

"I suppose." Of course, I didn't know for sure. I'd only been to Texas once, and that was a road trip across the panhandle on the way to Las Vegas. I don't even remember if I stopped while in Texas. If I did, it was only for gas or a trip to a restroom.

"The way I see things, we have three options. Option one is I come get you and we find a place nearby to live. We'd have to find a location with enough land to grow food, and near a good water source, and preferably within a short distance to a larger town so we can scrounge for materials or find people to trade with. Option two is I bring you back here. I've got a house in a valley with a productive garden, lots of game, and a stream right in the backyard."

"What's the third option?" Kayla asked.

"Option three is I pick you up and we randomly decide where we want to live."

"I like that option least of all," Kayla said.

"Agreed. Me too. So, what do you want?"

Kayla was silent for a moment. I didn't see her, but I assumed she had crinkled her nose and pursed her lips because she always made that face when she considered something important.

"I don't want to stay here. Because of my mom I only came back to be close to my folks, and since they're gone, I want to be too. Thinking about it, I certainly don't want to go north where it snows a lot. I couldn't handle the cold for half the year. The best option for me is to be at your place. Is that okay?"

"That's fine, whatever you want. Kayla, hold on a minute, okay? I'll be right back."

Without waiting for an answer, I set the phone down, scrambled into the living room, and flipped on the lights. I had a top-rate atlas with detailed pages for each state, so I removed the tome from the shelf, returned to the kitchen, and placed it on the table. I picked up the phone as I opened the book.

"Hey, I'm back, give me a minute,"

I thumbed through the atlas until I found the several pages for Texas. I found Dallas, and a second later I-45, and I traced my finger down the road until it settled on Rice. I turned back to the first page, which showed the entire country, checked the scale, and gave my best guess.

"From me to you is about twelve-hundred miles," I said.

"That far?" Kayla asked.

"Based on my best estimate. Might be farther or shorter based on the route I take."

"Would it be better if I met you halfway somewhere?"

I pondered over that idea for a moment, then discounted it. "I appreciate the offer, but I imagine you should stay put. It would be too difficult to plan a place to meet. The only contact we have now are these phones, and what would happen if they stopped working? We'd never find each other."

"I hadn't thought of that," she said. "I remember when I was a little kid I got lost at a mall when I was shopping with my mom. When I realized I lost her, I cried the whole time, and it took an entire hour until a security guard found me and got on the intercom to call her. That was only a mall. I can't even imagine trying to find a single person in an entire city, even if we managed to narrow that down to a specific location."

"There's also a matter of timing. If we met somewhere, there's no telling how long it would take either of us to get there. It's not like the trains are running on schedule."

"How long would it take you to get here?"

"Well, it would take me about an hour to get to the closest airport, maybe another three for the flight. I could be there this afternoon."

Kayla didn't say a word for a while, but after a couple of beats, she realized I was obviously joking.

"Funny man," she said. "Seriously, though."

"It's hard to say. If this were the before times, I could get in my car and drive there in a day. There are way too many variables. May take me a day, may take me a week or two."

"Okay," she said, but she didn't hide the disappointment in her voice. I didn't blame her. I could tell even over the phone she was hurting.

"Don't worry, I'll be there," I promised. "I'll need to do some travel prep once the sun comes up, and I'll be on the road by noon at the latest."

"Will you call every day? Tell me where you are?"

"Sure thing."

Kayla grew quiet again. I sensed she wanted to say something, but I didn't know what, and in the end, she didn't say.

"See you soon," she said, then closed the call.

I turned off the phone, set it down on the table and reflected on how I should go about this journey. I went back to the atlas, then state by state determined the best route to get there, which seemed to be to take I-81 into Tennessee, then I-40 to Little Rock, then take I-30 southwest to Dallas, then south on I-45 from there. On paper, it looked easy. Four main roads. It looked like a simple drive. Nothing to it.

I knew I wouldn't be able to sleep, so I threw on a pair of jeans and a sweatshirt, grabbed the barn keys, and sauntered outside into the night.

The light from the kitchen trailed off about halfway to the barn, but I found my way well enough to get there even if it was full dark. At the door, I slipped the key into the padlock, stepped through the door, and turned on the lights.

There were three vehicle choices to drive to Texas, but I didn't want to risk the pickup truck that I had converted to run on vegetable oil, and the Mustang I acquired recently still needed engine work and a new set of wheels. That left the old trusty mail truck. I thought my spine was going to shatter during the few hours it took me to drive it from Charlotte, but unless I procured something else, the mail truck was my only choice.

I let out a deep sigh, then turned my attention to the truck. I opened the back doors and saw it was empty, just as I expected it to be, so I set to work filling it up. Into the truck I put a few full gas cans, a hand pump I could use to siphon gas from other sources, and a few tools in case I had a breakdown along the way. Once I got the truck-related items in place, I pulled it out of the barn and parked it next to the back door. From the house, I added a few days' worth of food and water, a sleeping bag, and a backpack with a few changes of clothing. Almost as an afterthought, I added my 9mm and the rifle, with a couple of boxes of ammo for each, even though I had no intention of shooting at anything.

By the time I packed up, the sun was already over the trees and spreading along the valley. Although I was in a rush to leave, I took the time to make a small breakfast of the three remaining eggs I had, along with some venison jerky. I cleaned up the dishes, locked up the house and barn, got in the truck, and drove it up the mountain.

I didn't doubt that Pops was already up and about, and it didn't surprise me when I saw him appear at the door when I approached.

Right on schedule, as I left the truck, Frank and Dino ran over for head scratches and attention, which I gladly provided.

"What's up?" Pops asked as he settled into a chair.

"I'm leaving for a while. Think you can keep an eye on the place for me while I'm gone?"

"Going on vacation?" Pops asked, just before he broke into a round of laughter. "You going down to Florida beaches to work on your tan?" Pops teased.

"No. I wish. I'm going to Texas. Hoping to be back in a week, two at most."

"Texas? You said Texas?" Pops confirmed. Sometimes he was hard of hearing.

"Yep. Texas. Near Dallas."

"Why in the world would you go there?" he asked, as if he didn't believe me.

It took me a full fifteen minutes to tell him about Kayla's call and the plans we made. He didn't interrupt, but I could tell by the look on his face he didn't approve, either.

"Well?" I asked when I had finished, "what do you think?"

"I think you're a damn fool," he answered without a second of hesitation. "You can't imagine what it's like between here and there, or what trouble you could run into. Hell, if it weren't for me, you'd have died of starvation two months ago."

"I get that. I wouldn't have made it without you, that's true. You've been a mentor and a friend to me, but I need to do this. I'm all Kayla has left, and I can't leave her like this."

"I can't go with you," Pops said.

"I know, and I wouldn't expect you to. This is my quest."

That was an instance where the words sounded much cooler in my head than spoken aloud, and I confirmed it when Pops roared again with laughter.

"Your quest? You think you're King Arthur looking for the grail? Or Frodo returning a ring to Mount Doom?"

"No, I'm just trying to help a friend, and I hope you'll help me by watching my property."

Pops' countenance changed, and he looked more serious than I've ever seen him.

"You pack your gun?"

I nodded. "The pistol and the rifle."

"Good. I understand you don't want to use them, but if you have to, do it. And this ain't like the movies, son, where you have to shoot to kill. If you shoot to wound, that'll usually be a deterrent to a man. But it'll be best to avoid trouble, avoid cities and crowds of people if you can. A person is fine, two people may be fine, but any more than two in a group, and I'd be wary about it."

"I understand," I said.

"What else you got packed in there?" Pops said as he pointed at the truck.

I told him, and when I finished, he stepped into the house and returned a couple minutes later carrying a backpack.

"Take this," he said as he handed it to me. "It's a survival pack. Matches, a knife, thermal blanket, water filters, that kind of stuff. Put your ammo in there, and if you ain't got a holster, put the gun in there too. If you run into any trouble, make sure you got that pack and your rifle. Leave everything else. Don't be afraid to travel light, especially if you need to walk or find another way around. Got it?"

"Yeah, I got it," I said. I took a moment to rummage through the bag and see what it all contained. Then I did as Pops said and added my ammo and 9mm to the bag. I had never considered a holster, but I imagined I should find one at some point, since it seemed to be the thing everyone was wearing these days. We had devolved from 'don't wear white after Labor Day' to 'don't forget to strap on your holster'.

"I'll keep an eye out, especially the garden," Pops said with a wink.

"Thanks. I'll be back soon," I said.

"I hope so, son. I hope so."

Without another word, I got in the truck, did a U-turn, and went down the driveway. When I got near the road, I spotted a huge, downed tree blocking the driveway. I left the truck running, stepped off into the tree line, and cranked at a hand winch that lifted one end of the tree. Once the driveway was clear, I drove the truck through, then winched the tree back in place. A month after we removed the sign, we put the tree there to deter visitors, although neither one of us got any visitors to speak of. It's not that people didn't like us, since we both got along with the folks in town, but we were just too far out from town for anyone to stop in for a social call.

I got back in the truck, then hesitated. As I gripped the steering wheel, I got a pain in my stomach, like I ate a plate of bad mushrooms, but I assumed it was just jitters and the stress of setting out on this crazy adventure. If I was smart, I would turn around and go back home. Back to my garden, and Pops, and Dino and Frank. Back to the life I was rebuilding for myself. But then again, no one ever accused me of being smart, so I released my death grip from the steering wheel, hung a right onto the county road, and made a beeline for the interstate.

CHAPTER SEVEN

I was behind the wheel for perhaps a half hour when I realized I was missing something. Music. The radio turned up loud with Queen, or Springsteen, or whoever was keeping me company on a road trip. I didn't mind driving, but without a radio in the truck, the miles were lonely with only the sound of rushing wind blocking out the thoughts in my head. I'd be the first to admit that with every mile that passed from the comfort of home to the peril of the unknown, my stress level kicked up another notch, and since I had nothing as a distraction, my mind instinctively raced to thoughts of worse case scenarios. What if I was in a wreck or what if I didn't make it to Rice? What if I got all the way there and Kayla was gone, or worse yet, dead? If I made it, what if we didn't get back? What if I got kidnapped or killed? Although, I rationalized that if I got killed, that would end all my worries.

The tires hummed, and the wind whistled as I put miles behind me, and I realized it wouldn't be good enough, especially since I had another thousand miles to go.

Tennessee was approaching, and I pulled off the highway and into a small town to search for gas. I didn't like to get below a half tank if I could help it, and I certainly didn't want to break into my reserves so early into the trip. The town post office didn't have its own pumps, but there were a couple of trucks in the lot, and from those I siphoned enough gas to top off my tank. Across from the post office was a pawnshop, and I realized when I pulled up that it had been well-looted, but I stepped in regardless.

For the most part, anything of value had disappeared from the store, such as tools, weapons, and jewelry, but in the electronics section, I found what I wanted - a CD player, radio combination with built-in speakers that was referred to as a boombox back in the old days. I turned it on, and to my surprise, the red light on top lit up. It equally surprised me when I flipped open the cover and found a CD in the machine. I placed the cover back down and hit the play button. The disc started spinning, but no sound came from the speakers. It took only a second to discover the volume was all the way down, and when I turned it up, I heard Phil Collins from his Genesis days. That was good enough for me, so I turned off the player and turned it over to check what size batteries it took. D, like I assumed. I took the boombox with me as I checked every other electronic item left in the store, and in the end, I accumulated perhaps two dozen batteries in different sizes, including enough size Ds to change out the CD player once. I'd have to add batteries and CDs to the list of things to scrounge for whenever I stopped from now on.

Once I got back in the truck and found a spot on the floor where the CD player wouldn't slide around as I drove, I flipped it on, and set the volume to high. Now I was cruising in style, and my mood lifted considerably.

My mood lifted again when I passed into Tennessee, which meant I had only three more states to drive through, granted, two of them were long drives, but in my mind, the math worked out to twenty-five percent complete, and I had barely been on the road. I felt everything was going to be smooth sailing.

My smooth sailing ended when I got near downtown Knoxville. I was admiring the big gold ball leftover from some World's Fair when the interstate ended ahead of me. There was no warning, no signs, no idea at all, but as the road curved around on an overpass, the road disappeared to nothing. I slammed on the brakes, my seatbelt crushed against my chest, and Genesis stopped as the CD player rolled over and came to rest out of reach. Had it been night, or had I been going faster than fifty, I doubt I would have stopped in time. I undid my seatbelt, took a deep breath and walked to the edge and looked over. There were six cars and a semi on the roadway below, all of them smashed almost beyond recognition. I spotted one body, one unlucky person who ejected from the car upon impact with the ground, then the car somersaulted and landed on the lower half of them. It appeared to be a recent accident as the car was still smoldering and crows were dining on his entrails.

Once in the truck, I backed up a few feet and did a U-turn. I did another U-turn when I came to the first exit and left the interstate. Once I got to the end of the ramp, I hit the brakes again when a man stepped in front of the car brandishing a gun that he pointed at my eyes. I moaned, not at the threat, but rather that the boombox had done another roll. How much toppling would one machine take?

The man stepped around to the driver's door without leveling the gun. He looked to be a bit under six feet tall and wore Army fatigues from his cap down to his pants. I didn't see his feet, so I didn't know if he had Army-issued boots or sneakers. Not that it mattered. He looked like he was regular Army to me, complete with his name and service patches on his jacket.

I put my hands in the air, and while I did, I cursed myself for not keeping my own gun handy.

"Howdy," I said.

"Anyone else in the truck?"

"No, only me," I said.

Rather than take my word, the soldier opened the door and, with a practiced hand, pulled me from the seat and tossed me to the ground. I stayed face down as he checked the truck.

"Get up," he said.

As I did, he slung his rifle over his shoulder.

"Sorry about that. You can't be too careful these days," he said.

I agreed but didn't say so.

He came right to the point. "I could use some food, water, and a ride."

I looked at him cautiously.

"Look, I'm not a thief. I don't want to hurt you. I just need some help."

After a quick consideration, I believed him. He could have killed me three times already, but didn't. Surely, I could spare some supplies in exchange for my life. I went to the back, opened the doors, and presented the soldier with a bottle of water, a jar of peaches, and a small plastic baggie of venison jerky. He took them all, downed half of the water in one gulp, then started in on the jerky.

"How about a ride?" he asked.

"Where are you headed?" I asked.

He took a drink before answering. "Chattanooga."

"Sorry," I said, "I'm headed to Texas via I-40, otherwise I'd be happy to take you along."

"No, you're not. Nashville is half-burned to the ground, and the bridges are all out around Memphis. You'll never get over the Mississippi River there."

That I didn't believe. "How do you know?"

The soldier pointed to the patch on his arm that read U.S. Army. "I have it on real good authority. When they implemented Marshall Law, most of the people in the larger cities in the country were... hesitant to comply. Let's say things got really rough in a lot of places, and I'd recommend you avoid as many metropolises as you can."

I didn't know if I believed him, and my doubt must have shown on my face.

"Here, look." He set the food on the truck's hood, then pulled a map from his jacket pocket and opened it. The wind started to take it, so he put it down and set the water bottle on one corner and the peaches on another. The map was of the southeastern United States, with the northernmost states being Tennessee and North Carolina, and the westernmost states being Arkansas and Louisiana. What caught my immediate attention was the red Xs that covered several cities. Nashville and Memphis in Tennessee, New Orleans, Tampa, Miami, Jacksonville, Little Rock, Atlanta. Charlotte. I noticed Mississippi and Alabama were clean.

"These mean what I think they do?" I asked.

"Does a red X ever mean anything good?" came the reply.

Charlotte? I came from there. It was rough, but not bad enough to deserve the X. Or did it? Either way, I must have made it out just in time.

"When did this all happen?"

"Over the last one to six months."

"What about other parts of the country? New York, or Washington, or L.A.?"

"With all the unrest in Washington, that was the first city to go."

"What about Dallas?"

The soldier nodded. "Yep, that too."

My heart dropped a bit, but I hoped Kayla was far enough away to avoid the disaster.

"I guess I need to find another route, then. Chattanooga it is. There's only one seat, so you'll have to sit on the floor," I said.

The soldier nodded, gathered up the map and food, slipped into the truck, and got as comfortable as he could. "Turn left. About a mile south of here, turn right on Highway 11. We can pick up the interstate to Chattanooga about thirty miles west of here."

I started the engine, then followed his directions as he dined on peaches and jerky.

"I'm Collins, by the way. Thank you for the food. I haven't eaten in a couple of days."

"I'm Baker," I said. "What's in Chattanooga?" I asked.

"Hopefully, my wife and kids. I've been trying to get back for weeks now. I've been walking and hitching rides for about three weeks."

"Where are you coming from? Did you get a discharge?" I asked, making small talk.

"You really don't want to know, Baker. Let's just say I was a part of the cleanup crew on one of those X's, and what I experienced made me lose my stomach for the Army, and I wasn't the only one. I got my discharge when a soldier in my unit had enough and put a bullet into the back of the CO's head, and that was the end of that."

I didn't know how to respond, so I drove in silence. Eventually, I met up with Interstate 75 and turned left toward Chattanooga.

"Where are you headed?" Collins asked.

"A small town south of Dallas. There's a girl who—"

I stood on the brakes for the third time that day. I heard Collins mutter an expletive after I saw his head connect with the wall.

"Sorry. Bridge out. What's with all the bridges out?"

Collins got to his feet and looked out the windshield. "Standard military procedure to prevent people from going too far. Turn around, get off at the first exit, and head east. There's another bridge over the river in the town near here."

I did as I was told, and Collins repeated his expletive when he realized that the alternate bridge was out, too.

"Hold on, maybe we'll get lucky here."

There was a boat ramp nearby, and at the end of the ramp I spotted what looked to be a barge, and on the end of that barge sat a man in a chair engrossed in a book. I turned the truck into the parking area, and Collins and I jumped out and approached the man. As we got closer, I could tell that he wasn't reading at all, but rather, was in a mid-afternoon nap.

"Hello? Excuse me?" I said.

There was no response from the man, so Collins rapped the hull of the boat with his gun. At the sound of the clank, the man opened his eyes and focused on Collins. He shifted ever so slightly in his chair, and I noticed the pistol hidden under his right leg. When Collins returned his rifle over his shoulder, the man relaxed, then smiled.

"You need across the river?" he asked.

"Yes," I answered.

"What you got to offer in trade?"

"I got some food, water, not much else."

The man dog-eared the book and dropped it on the deck. "I have food and water. You got anything else?"

The only thing of value I had were my weapons and ammo, but I wasn't about to give those up. "Nope."

"Sorry. No ride," the man said, then leaned to pick up the book.

I turned to leave, but Collins stayed firm.

"Where'd you serve, old timer?" Collins asked.

"How'd you know I did?" the old man asked. He leaned forward in his chair, removed his dirty Atlanta Braves baseball cap, and pushed his long gray hair back and replaced the cap. He stood and spit over the side and into the river. I watched as it hit the water and saw something from below grab it and go.

Collins nodded at the side of the barge. I looked and saw a canvas duffel bag. The old man followed Collins' gaze as well and spotted what had drawn his attention.

"Bah, everyone's got one of them. I picked it up at the surplus store," the old man said.

"No, you didn't," Collins countered.

The two men stared at each other for a full minute before the old man finally broke out into a grin and laughed. "Shit. Okay, you got me. I did two tours in the Gulf. Back in the good old days, when we went to war on the other side of the world."

"I'll bet that was tough. Especially being away from family," Collins said.

The old man hesitated, and something in his eyes told me he was remembering just what that had been like. He didn't answer, but gave us half a nod.

Collins pointed across the river toward the south. "That's what I'm trying to do. Get to Chattanooga. Back to my family."

Collins stopped speaking and waited for a reply. It took almost two minutes, then finally the old man moved his chair to the edge of the barge. "I guess we can't let the river here stand in the way of you reuniting with your kin. Drive that thing aboard."

I returned to the truck, Collins stepped to the side, and the old man used hand signals to make sure I centered the truck on the barge. When I did, I put it in Park. I thought Collins was going to jump back in with me, but he didn't. Instead, he made small talk with the old man while he busied himself preparing the barge for sail. I felt a strong jerk, then we moved away from the bank. I thought perhaps there were engines moving us, but when I looked again, I noticed that the whole thing operated by a guide rope and a winch. Slowly we made our way across the river, and since I pictured the worst-case scenario of us capsizing and ending up in the water, I closed my eyes and practiced some deep breathing exercises. Ten minutes later, I felt another bump. I opened my eyes and saw the old man ahead of me on the bank waving at me to drive off the barge. I did, then stopped on the bank and waited for Collins. In the side mirror I watched as they shook hands, then Collins jumped back into the truck, and I followed his directions back to the interstate.

"Nice of him to let us through," I said.

Collins nodded. "Yeah, we got lucky there. I was hoping I wouldn't have to shoot him."

I turned my head to look at Collins, trying to determine if he was kidding, but I could only spot enough of him to determine he'd started back in on the jerky. Getting the hint, I drove in silence for an hour, and when I saw the sign that Chattanooga was only a few miles away, I brought it to Collins' attention and he got to a crouch, hung onto the back of my seat, and gave me directions until I at last pulled into the driveway of a ranch-style house with bars on the windows and front door. I saw the curtain move by what I thought was a bedroom window, then the end of a shotgun poked out. I got out of the truck and put my hands in the air. Collins got out behind me, but his hands up as well, and took a step toward the window.

"Baby? Hey, it's me. I'm home." Collins dropped took off his hat and sunglasses and let them drop to the ground.

He stood statue still for what seemed like forever. Then I saw the shotgun barrel retreat, and a minute later the front door opened, and a woman ran out of the house. Collins moved toward her, and when they met and embraced, I turned around to give them a moment to enjoy their reunion.

"Hey," Collins said to me.

I turned back around and saw they were arm in arm, looking in my direction. Collins waved me over, and I joined them.

"This is Taylor," he said.

Taylor released her grip on Collins and gave me a hug. She stood an inch taller than me, had long blond hair, and smelled of floral soap. I accepted the tentative hug, then she released me and returned to Collins' side.

"Come on in. Have a meal. You can stay the night and get a fresh start in the morning," Collins said.

I protested at first, but regardless of the excuses I made to get back on the road, Taylor dismissed them all, and before I knew it, they ushered me into the house and showed me the guest room, which included its own shower, complete with its own floral soap. I relented and hunkered down for the night.

CHAPTER EIGHT

When I left the next morning, I did so with three things: the map Collins had showed me the day before, his spare Army jacket, complete with his name and American flag patches, and a small tin of chocolate chip cookies. On the way in, I spotted a used bookstore from the interstate, so the first stop I made when I left Collins was there. As was the case with just about everywhere these days, the people had torn the doors off the hinges, and they sat discarded in the parking lot. I grabbed my gun, locked the truck, and entered the building. When I stepped in, I marveled at the place. It looked like in its heyday to be a remarkable store. I wandered around the first floor where I found eight six-foot tall shelving units that ran the width of the building that were dedicated to movies, video games, board games, and puzzles. Some shelves were empty, like there wasn't a puzzle or video game to be found. Others had the merchandise scattered all over the floor, and others remained untouched. Past those shelves were the books. There were fourteen long shelves, subdivided into cubby holes in which books sat, categorized by genre and alphabetized by author. I did a quick run through the fiction and picked out three books at random. Then I spotted the stairs to the mezzanine level that took up the three outer walls of the building. There, I found what I had come for: more CDs. Unfortunately, with all the brake slamming, Phil Collins and Genesis had suffered enough damage so that the disc wouldn't get more than four bars into the first song before it skipped.

The bins I reached first contained old-fashioned vinyl records, and they stretched the entire length of the wall. When I turned the corner, I found the CDs. Like the puzzles, people had picked through them pretty good, and in the end, I walked away with only an old George Strait CD, a classic from John Coltrane, and the soundtrack from the musical *Wicked*. I took my six new items back downstairs, and with my gun drawn, peeked out the front door to ensure no one was around. The coast was clear, so I slipped out of the building, climbed into my truck, and drove off.

My next goal was to make Birmingham, Alabama, which, by interstate, was normally only two hours away. Instead, the night before, Collins and I worked out an alternate route where I would follow I-24 and take that only as far as where it met up with Highway 72, just north of the Alabama border. From there, I would pick up Highway 79 in Scottsboro and continue southwest to Birmingham. It added at least another hour to the trip, but the benefits of not being exposed on the interstate the whole way, and going through more towns where I could resupply as needed more than made up for the hours' time loss.

The plan worked well. For forty minutes, that is, until I reached the spot where the interstate crossed the Tennessee River. Once again, I found a crater, broken concrete, and rebar where the bridge should have been. Lucky for me, there was an offramp only a few hundred yards behind me, so I drove over the median, headed to the crossroad, and left the interstate. I drove down the ramp, pulled off the road, and dug out my atlas. The road I was currently on followed the river until it met back up with the highway I needed a few miles to the west. Although, as my finger followed the planned route, the road crossed the river at two spots. One, where the highway passed over a small bay, and the second where it crossed the river proper. I shook my head in exasperation, then set to work finding a route that avoided both interstate and major river crossings. It took almost twenty minutes of study, but finally had a route that met my requirements.

I put the postal truck in gear, did yet another U-turn, and got back on the interstate and headed back toward Chattanooga. When I-24 met up with I-59 as I dipped down into Georgia, I took the new interstate and got off at the first exit I came to. I turned right, drove past a burned down gas station, and a couple of miles later turned onto a Georgia highway. From there, I only needed to make one turn a few miles up the road until I came to the Alabama state line, where that road would turn into Alabama Highway 75, which I planned to follow straight into Birmingham. By my calculations, my easy two-hour drive had tripled in time.

I sighed, but let my frustration pass when I remembered choices got dictated differently now, and the concept of fate being in one's own hands was now a mixture of circumstance and luck. Needing a brief break, I slowed the truck, then stopped in the middle of the road. I leaned over, removed the Genesis CD from the boombox, tossed it without regard into the back, and replaced it with the John Coltrane disc. When the dulcet tones of the saxophone rushed from the speakers, I turned up the volume, took a cleansing breath, and drove on.

My trip through the northwest corner of Georgia was blessedly uneventful. My alternate route took me mostly past houses and a handful of churches. I eventually passed one small section at a crossroads that had a tax service, a convenience store, and a food pantry. The pantry looked boarded shut. The convenience store had a Ford F-150 stuck halfway in the building, and there was no longer a need for tax services, so I kept driving.

Close to the state border, I spotted a gas station. I checked the gauge, noticed it hovering just above a half tank, slowed, and pulled into the station. I pulled up to the pump farthest from the small market and hesitated before getting out. Something didn't look quite right. Everything in the area looked too… normal. The building ahead looked to be in pristine shape. No broken or boarded windows, and they were all clean. I looked over and noticed the pumps had power, and the entire lot was devoid of trash or any debris. I looked back at the building. The sign in the front window claimed I could win eight-hundred million in the long-defunct lottery. I left the engine running, got out of the truck, and at a snail's pace approached the pump, staying as vigilant as a mouse traversing a field filled with hawks and rattlesnakes.

I looked at the pump. Gas at this location sold for an even fifty bucks per gallon, but that didn't bother me since I had a pocket full of credit cards. They were another thing that made little sense in the new world. If you found a pump or vending machine that accepted cards and still had power, as long as the card was within the limits, it still worked, as if the credit card companies were the last vestige of the old world. From my back pocket, I pulled a Visa issued in the name of a woman I'd never met and tapped it against the reader. As I waited, the little display said it was processing. I stood in the sun patiently waiting for the transaction to go through when I felt something whiz by my cheek and impact the truck behind me. Right there in the painted field of blue that made up the eagle's neck was a fresh bullet hole. On instinct, I ducked, dropped the gas hose, and ran around to the door. In the seconds it took me to get in the truck and throw it into Drive, I heard two additional impacts. I stomped on the accelerator and sped out of the lot, leaving a layer of rubber behind me. I flew down the highway, almost in a panic. A spasm hit and I jerked the wheel to avoid hitting something in the road, over-corrected, spun in a complete circle and slammed on the brakes. Dead ahead was a sign welcoming me to sweet home Alabama.

For almost an hour and a half, I drove down the highway, hyper-vigilant and running on adrenaline. I slowed to a reasonable speed when I got to the city of Albertville, and I was glad I had the truck at a slow pace when a girl, no more than nine, bounded out into the street chasing a rubber ball. I hit the brakes and lurched forward in my seat as I came to an abrupt stop. The CD player took yet another tumble, and Coltrane's sax went silent. Following the girl was who I assumed was the father, who rushed after her and scooped her up in his arms, then turned and waved at me. As I waved back, he motioned for me to follow him, and I turned into a grocery store parking lot. I swung the truck around, so it was facing the way out, kept the motor running, slipped my gun into my pocket, and stepped out onto the concrete.

The second my shoes hit the pavement, the man put his daughter on the ground and took two quick steps toward me. I stepped back into the side of my truck and fumbled for my gun but couldn't grab it in time. In seconds, the man was upon me, gathered me up in a crushing bear hug and kissed me on both cheeks.

"Thank you. Thank you so much for stopping," the man exclaimed as he let me go. "I keep telling her that roads are still dangerous even though there's not as many cars on them. But she refuses to listen." He stepped back and took the girl's little hand in his.

"Yeah. Um, kids can be like that, I guess," I said. I took a moment to get my first good look at the man. He stood two inches shorter than me. He had jet black hair, a thin mustache and beard, and was thin enough I probably could have wrapped my fingers around his wrist and still touch thumb to forefinger. Based on his skin tone, I suspected he had some Hispanic heritage in his background, although I didn't detect an accent when he spoke.

"I'm Marcos. This is Lucia. Lucia, say hi."

I watched as the girl took a step backward, then gave me a greeting in such a quiet voice I barely caught it.

"Baker," I said. "Nice to meet you."

"Please, would you join us for a meal?" Marcos asked, nodding as he did so.

He looked me in the eye, waiting for a response, then let out a hearty laugh. "No, my friend. I'm not a rover. You don't need to worry about me. Come, join us. We're right over there."

Marcos turned around and pointed to the far end of the parking lot, closer to the grocery store. There, I saw a large blue tent, under which was a hive of action. I couldn't tell what everyone was doing from a distance, but I could tell based on the column of smoke rising in the air that some of it involved a grill.

I thought about it for a microsecond. He could have invited me to my demise, or a fantastic lunch, but I wouldn't know which one was it until I went over. In the end, I didn't need to answer because my stomach did it for me when it growled loud enough for all three of us to hear. Marcos smiled, and Lucia giggled at the noise coming from my empty belly.

"So that's a yes then," Marcos said. "Come."

I was about to respond when my phone trilled. "I need to get this. You go ahead and I'll be right there," I said.

Marcos nodded and led Lucia away while I climbed back into the truck and grabbed the phone.

"Hello? Kayla?"

"Baker?"

"Yes, I'm here. What's going on? Everything okay?"

A bit of static came through the line, then I caught the last half of her sentence.

"Can you repeat that?" I asked.

"I said I had to leave," Kayla said. Her voice came in loud and clear, and it sounded to me like she was yelling into the phone.

"Leave where?" I asked.

"Home. A gang came through. They killed people, Baker. And burned down almost every building."

I shivered at the news.

"Are you okay?" I asked.

"Yes. I moved into the shed and hid there until last night. Then I left town."

"Where did you go?"

"I'm just east of Shreveport, Louisiana. I traveled all night and found an old barn to settle down in for a while. Where are you?"

"I just got into Albertville, Alabama."

"Where's that?" she asked.

"Northeast of Birmingham. I've been encountering delays, so I'm not making as many miles as quickly as I thought I would."

"What should we do? Where should we meet?" she asked.

"Hold on."

I consulted my trusty atlas to determine what a good midpoint would be.

"Do you think you can make it to Jackson, Mississippi? That's the largest city halfway between us at this point."

"Hold on," Kayla said.

Through the phone, I caught some pages turning, and Kayla hummed to herself. Another nervous habit I remembered she had.

"That's only about two hundred miles from here. I think I can do that," she said.

"Okay. It's three hundred for me, so you'll probably beat me there," I said. "We should check in every day. What time would work for you?"

There came another momentary pause. "Can we do twice a day? Eight and eight?" she said.

"That works for me. I'll call you. If you don't answer, I'll try every thirty minutes. If I don't call, you call me every thirty minutes. Okay by you?"

"Yes. Okay. I need to get some sleep. I'll talk to you tonight."

"Sure. Talk to you later. Bye."

"Baker?" she blurted, before I had a chance to disconnect the call.

"Yes?"

Kayla exhaled, but she didn't speak for a moment. "Be careful," she said finally. Kayla disconnected the call before I could wish her the same.

I stared at the dead phone in my hand for a good two minutes before I at last stowed it back in the five-gallon pail I was using to hold random items. I looked to see if Marcos was still in view, but he wasn't. After I righted the CD player, I put the truck in gear and drove slowly across the lot. When I got to within twenty yards of the tent, I parked the truck, got out, and locked it. As I walked toward the tent, Marcos came out with a plate of food and greeted me before I even got there. I took the plate and looked at it. On it were two hot dogs, baked beans, and an ear of sweet corn.

"You want mints?" Lucia asked, peeking out from behind her father.

"Mints?" I asked.

"She means condiments. Ketchup, mustard, relish," Marcos said as he handed me a fork.

"I'd love some ketchup," I said.

Marcos nodded and waved at me to follow him, which I did. Just inside the tent, he led me to an unoccupied picnic table, and we sat. Lucia disappeared and returned thirty seconds later with plastic bottles in red and yellow, and a small jar of pickle relish. She set them on the table, then disappeared again.

"So, where you headed?" Marcos asked as I dressed my dogs. "You're not from around here. Passing through?"

Just as he spoke, I bit into one of the hot dogs. Growing up, I was never much of a fan of the common hot dog. Even though they were associated with being a special treat while at carnivals and baseball games, I still never felt compelled to have one. Today, though, biting into that meat stick was the closest I'd ever come to a religious experience. My teeth busted through the casing with a pop, and the mix of pork, ketchup, mustard, and dill pickle relish almost overloaded my taste buds. I downed the dog in four bites before turning my attention back to Marcos.

"I'm going to Jackson, Mississippi to pick up a friend, then I'm taking her back to my farm in Virginia," I said.

Marcos offered me a cup of water. I drank it. It felt cool and looked clear, and I detected an ice cube. Clearly, things were going well in Albertville, Alabama.

"You have any problems with the rovers up there?" Marcos asked.

"Rovers? That's the second time you've used that term. What are they?" I asked as I picked up a spoon and started making my way through the baked beans.

"We've heard stories of bad people banding together and terrorizing communities. They go in like locusts to strip it bare. Take all the food and fuel. Harass anyone they want. Often leaving nothing but death and fire in their wake before they move on to the next town."

I reflected for a moment and wondered if that was what Kayla had experienced.

I shook my head. "No. But I live a fair distance from a town. I'm out in the boonies on the side of a mountain."

"Good. You should stay that way. It's safer."

"Do you know how large the groups are?" I asked.

Marcos sat back in his seat and took a drink from his own cup. From the way his nose crinkled, I expected he had something besides water in his cup. "As few as three or four, as many as a hundred. Evil doesn't have a set size."

I nodded. "Where are you getting your information from?"

Marcos threw a thumb over his shoulder. "We've got a couple of guys who were shortwave radio freaks before the end times came. Now they're two of the most important people in town. They're on shift every day, getting news and keeping us updated with what's going on all over the country. So far, we're talking with a half dozen communities. As far as South Dakota to the north and New Mexico out west. The funny thing is they're all smaller ones like us. I would've thought that we'd heard from a city like Denver or New Orleans, but not so. It seems not everyone has picked up on the shortwave idea yet."

"I guess not," I said as I put my fork down. My stomach turned as I thought about all the cities with the red X over them on the map in my truck. I looked back at my plate. I still had half a hot dog to go, and I hadn't touched the corn yet. My stomach did a slow roll. I was no longer hungry, but I knew I needed to clean the plate. I needed the calories, and I didn't want to insult my host.

"Are you still planning on going? To meet your friend in Jackson?" Marcos asked. "It might be safer to turn around and go home."

"I would love to go back home, Marcos. But the thing is, I made a promise. One I must see through."

CHAPTER NINE

After I finished my meal, Marcos took me around and introduced me to over a dozen people. I thought it a gracious gesture, and I couldn't help but notice how in this small cross section of America people rallied together. Here, underneath this tent, several races and cultures blended as if several hundred years' worth of infighting had never happened. To paraphrase one person I talked to, who was sleeping with who, and the different amounts of melanin that people produced took a back seat when it came to the needs of shelter, food, and keeping the lights on. They had come together as a community, and I had half a thought of staying with them. I knew I couldn't since I'd made the promise. I'd given my word, and when it came to Kayla, I intended to keep it.

When the sun started to slant more toward the west, I felt the urge of the road beckoning to me. I gave thanks to several people, and Marcos walked me back to my car.

"Remember, my friend, if you run into the rovers, they'll take whatever you have of value, and if you're lucky, they'll leave you only with your life. Avoid them if you can," Marcos said. He brought me into an embrace, let me go, uttered something in Spanish I took as a blessing, and turned and headed back under the tent.

I unlocked the truck, got in, and made sure I still had everything I stopped with. Nothing looked out of order, so I started the engine, gave a last wave through the windshield, and pulled away. Before I was even out of the parking lot, I noticed that at some point during lunch, someone had filled the gas tank. When I pulled in, I was at a quarter tank, and now the little red needle hung above the full line.

I took one look back before I pulled out onto the road, then continued southwest to Birmingham. As I drove, I mulled over what Marcos had told me about the rovers. Eventually, I pulled over into an abandoned used car lot and parked out of view from the street. I took stock of what I had up front with me, which wasn't much. There was my CD player, CDs, and a plastic bag of batteries for the player, along with my trusty atlas and a couple of state maps I'd picked up along the way, both of which were states I wasn't currently in and didn't plan on visiting anytime soon. I stepped to the rear of the truck and opened the back door. In there, I glimpsed the backpack Pops gave me, my rifle, my duffel that held my clothes for a trip. Two spare tires sat stacked one on another, and next to that were a car jack and tire iron. I also had two small cardboard boxes back there, each about the size of a case of printer paper. The first held my provisions. Jarred fruits from Pops, canned vegetables, a couple cans of Spam, and an ample supply of jerky. The other box held random tools that I would use in the event of a breakdown. Also in that box was an old rusty gun. I'd found it somewhere and tossed it in the box for some reason instead of throwing it away.

I stood for a moment, staring at the stash, until I finally made a decision and reached for the backpack. In it, I added my handgun, my satellite phone, and half of the credit cards I had on me. I was about to step away when I dug the jerky out of the food box and added it to the backpack as well. Satisfied, I zipped up the backpack, grabbed the rifle, and made my way to the side of the truck opposite the steering wheel, which was on the wrong side of the vehicle compared to every other car on the road. The slide door had never worked, so with equal parts welding, ingenuity, auto body filler, and paint, Pops and I had constructed a small hidden compartment beneath the truck. It wasn't large enough to hold a person, but it was plenty big to hold my backpack and rifle, so I secreted both items inside and closed the hidden panel that attached via strong rare earth magnets.

With my important items hidden, I moved to shut the back door, but at the last moment, I grabbed the old, rusted gun and took it with me to the front. I tossed it on the floor next to the CD player and closed the door. Before I shifted into Drive, I picked up the atlas and double checked my route. From Albertville, it was a straight shot to Birmingham. There I'd pick up some local roads which would eventually connect with U.S. 11, which would take me to Tuscaloosa. From there, I would follow a few highways that paralleled the interstate through Meridian, Mississippi, right on to Jackson. I didn't bother to calculate the time, since I'd discovered when I left my home that time had become somewhat fluid and unreliable.

Once I knew where I needed to go, I pressed the button to start the CD player, and listened to music as I drove down the road. My belly was full, as was my fuel tank, so I hadn't a care in the world as I drove. I didn't encounter a single other car, and noticed only one other person who was on horseback trying to lasso a cow. The sky was bright blue, the temperature warm, and if I was making the drive under different circumstances, it might have made for a nice leisurely ride.

I slowed my pace when I saw the sign welcoming me to the city, and I pulled over to the edge of the road to check my atlas. Fortunately, the book included a map subset of the city, and it seemed an easy enough route to get from where I was to where I wanted to be on the opposite side of town. All I needed to do was follow the signs. I had two options. One was to drive through town as fast as possible and hope I didn't run anyone down, and the other was slowing it down and taking my time while I scanned ahead for potential problems. I went with the latter.

I was on a two-lane road, but I stayed right down the middle, like my truck was Pac-Man gobbling up dots while I looked for ghosts. As the buildings grew larger and closed around me, I kept my head on a swivel, searching for potential problems. I felt my chest tighten, then realized I'd been holding my breath as I navigated the streets of the downtown area. It appeared I didn't need to worry, as there wasn't a soul to be seen. The only time I slowed my steady pace was when a mama cat with a kitten held by the scruff meandered across the street without a care in the world.

My eyes wandered to a faded brown National Park Service sign that directed me to the Birmingham Civil Rights National Monument. In the old world, it would have tempted me to take the detour and check out the site. Those were the days I loved visiting the national parks. I even had an annual park pass that got me into all of them, and I loved exploring the ones known for scenic beauty just as much as the lesser-known parks that offered no scenery but plenty of history instead. But those days were over, and I didn't think twice about stopping.

The sign distracted me enough that I barely noticed the man dressed like an old-west sheriff who stepped off of the curb and pointed a shotgun in my direction. He screamed "yee-haw" at the top of his lungs, then pulled the trigger. I jerked the wheel to the right and a second after the boom from the gun echoed in my ears, I heard the pellets hit the truck. A few made it through the open window, and one grazed my shoulder, causing me to cry out in pain as I stomped on the accelerator. I lurched forward, then saw another cowboy step out into the middle of the street. As he raised his gun, rather than veer away, I steered straight for him. He pulled the trigger a second before I caught him with the front bumper. The windshield starred, and the truck lurched as I hit the man. In the side mirror, I saw him roll a few times and then come to a stop, face down in the street.

Two more cowboys ran out of a building to my right, and I instinctively turned the wheel hard to the left to go down a side street. I'd turned the corner, my foot still on the gas. Dead ahead was a tanker truck parked sideways and blocking both lanes of the road. My foot flew from the gas to the brake, and I yanked on the wheel. Outside the broken windshield, the big tanker loomed closer as the brakes screamed and the tires laid rubber on the road. My truck finally turned, and I realized my actions fell short as the brick wall of a building came into view. The last thought that went through my head before I lost consciousness was they'd ambushed me.

As I came to, I felt myself being dragged by my arms. I struggled to open my eyes and found although my right one worked fine, blood seeped into the left eye the second I tried to open it. I relied only on my good eye, and I saw they were dragging me across the street from where my truck had run into the red brick wall of the First State Bank. As a couple of cowboys started rummaging through my truck in a free-for-all, I struggled to break free from the arm hold my captors held me in. They only strengthened their grip as they dragged me across the concrete like an old rug.

We entered another building, and the men picked me up and slammed me into a chair. One left, and one stepped right in front of me. Rather than a cowboy, this one appeared to be dressed in a biker motif. He wore blue jeans, a T-shirt with a picture of a middle finger being extended, and a black leather vest, complete with a fringed bottom. He looked like he'd had a splendid physique at one time, but although he was still a large man, his muscles looked to be more flab than toned. On his head we wore a biker bandanna with red flames and black skulls, under which his long greasy hair peeked out. He was one of those guys who had a tough time growing facial hair and resented it, so he wore a short mustache and a stubble for a beard.

"You a fag?" the burly man asked.

"What?" I wasn't sure if I'd heard him right.

"Are. You. A. Fag?" he repeated, punctuating his words. "You know. A homo."

I shook my head. When I did, a drop of warm goo fell onto my cheek.

"You're bleeding," the man said. He stepped from my field of vision, and as he did, I touched my forehead above my left eye and felt the stickiness there. The man returned with a towel that he threw me. I used it to wipe the blood from around my eye, then pressed it against my head.

"Thanks," I said.

"So, now. You a homo?" he asked again.

"No. I'm not. I'm straight as an arrow," I said honestly.

"You sure?" he asked.

I nodded again. "Of course."

"You from the gov'ment?"

"No. Why would you think that?" I asked.

"Why you drive a mail truck?"

Why did they send an idiot to do this interrogation? I thought. "I stole it. It's what I use to get around. Blends in nice."

The man considered my point for a moment. "Where you goin'?"

"Jackson, Mississippi. I'm picking up my girlfriend there," I answered, seeing no reason to lie about it, and only stretching the truth a little. Kayla wasn't my girlfriend, but I hope he'd make the connection that having a girlfriend would make me not gay.

"She Black or Mexican?" he asked.

"What?"

In response to my query, he pulled a revolver from his belt and pointed it at my face.

"You must be real hard of hearing if I need to keep repeatin' questions for you. Is your woman Black or Mexican?"

I put my hand out in front of me. "Please. I'm sorry. I'm a little slow from hitting my head. My girlfriend is White."

"Is she a Jew?" he asked.

That I didn't know the answer to. I'd never asked. I doubted it, since she never mentioned being Jewish, and she always sent me a winter solstice card every year. "Nope. She's a blond-haired, blue-eyed, all-American Christian girl."

That seemed to satisfy his curiosity about my love life and stepped away to look outside the plate-glass window.

"You want to watch out for that one," someone whispered to me. I looked to my left and saw a man with a skinny face and round, wire-rimmed glasses. He looked to be about sixty and like he'd stepped right out of the *American Gothic* painting. "He's strong and dumb. That's a terrible combination."

"What is he going to do with us?" I asked.

The man shrugged. "I don't know. I've been sitting here for three days."

"How'd you end up here?" I asked.

"Same way you did. They chased me around the corner, and I stopped when I almost ran into that truck."

"They get anyone else?"

"Not alive. There was a Black couple. They shot them in the street without question. And there was another woman who came through here. I can't tell you what she looked like. All I heard were the screams when they dragged her off."

"What about —"

"Shh. They're coming back."

The man sat back, relaxed in his chair, and I did the same. A few seconds later, two of the cowboys entered the building. One stepped quickly toward me and stopped, pointing at my face close enough that I could see the grime under his fingernails.

"This one killed Bobby," the man said.

Before anyone could do anything, the man slapped me across the face. On impact, my head recoiled backward and slammed against the wall. My vision blurred for a moment, and when it came back into focus, I saw the other cowboy rush forward and pulled the man away.

"I know. I saw it. Because I was there, remember? As far as I'm concerned, he did me a favor. Bobby was an idiot, plain and simple."

"But still, it was Bobby."

"Forget it, Mac. Bobby's dead. But I don't want this one dead quite yet."

Mac glared at me, then left the building, pushing the building's door so hard that it pulled the top hinge free. He continued on, full of rage, fighting with the door until he busted it free completely and tossed it into the street.

"Mac's real mad," the biker said to the cowboy.

"He sure is. It'll pass, just like a summer storm. Don't you worry about it, son."

The cowboy turned his attention to me. Under his brown ten-gallon hat, he wore salt and pepper hair and a face chiseled by time and a lifetime of manual labor.

"Here's how this goes," the cowboy said. "You're going to sit tight right here until I decide what to do with you."

"If it's all the same to you, I'd much rather just get in my truck and go. I was just passing through town, anyway. I'll be on my way and avoid this town in this future."

The cowboy shook his head. "Don't work that way. I'm the boss here and I decide. I can already see you've got some redeeming qualities, so we need to determine what benefit you'd be around here."

"What do you mean by redeeming qualities?" I asked.

He grinned at me. "You're part of the master race, my brother." He slapped me playfully across the cheek. "Now you just sit tight, and I'll come back later, and we'll talk more."

The cowboy left and the biker man stayed behind with us, his attention drawn to the men still ransacking my truck. I assumed in the short time I'd been in here; they'd already stripped it clean.

I removed the towel from my head, turned it over, then dabbed my head with it. Based on the amount of blood, I could tell the worst of the bleeding was over, and I was happy not to need actual medical attention.

"What's your plan?" the old man whispered to me.

"I'm getting out of town the first chance I see. They ever take you out of here?"

"Only to go to the bathroom, which is down that hallway to your right. Otherwise, I sit here all day with Bubba watching over me."

"What about at night?"

"It depends. Sometimes they post a guard all night, sometimes they lock me in the toilet."

"So that's the plan, then. I wait until they take you to the toilet, then I leave."

"That's not going to work," the man said.

"Why not?"

He dropped his voice an octave. "Because if you don't take me with you, I'm going to tell them what you're going to do, and they'll take you outside and shoot you in the gutter."

I nodded that I understood. I wanted to protest, but honestly, I couldn't blame the old-timer for wanting to get out, too. "Okay. So, we come up with a plan where we both escape."

"Good."

"What else can you tell me?" I asked.

"Well, just about every day Bubba drinks too much lemonade."

I looked over at the man staring out the window and for the first time; I noticed the three one-gallon jugs near his feet. One was empty, the others filled with a yellow liquid I assumed was lemonade.

"What happens when he needs to pee?" I asked.

"He locks the front door so I can't escape, then he uses the toilet."

I looked at the front door. Or at least the hole where the door used to be before Mac threw it into the street.

"I think I have a plan," I said.

CHAPTER TEN

I stayed seated and unmoving, but kept on full alert, watching what was happening around me. Bubba paid more attention to the outside world than to his two captives, which was fine with me. He also stood in front of the window, which would have been a problem were I in the other seat, but where I was, I had a view straight out the front door. I noticed that my truck was no longer the hive of activity it had been. The back door was open, and I could tell from where I sat that they'd cleaned it out. My duffel and random boxes were gone. As long as they hadn't discovered my secret compartment, I thought I'd still be in good shape.

As he watched, Bubba drank from the gallon jugs. When he was a quarter way through the second one, he turned around, looking uncomfortable. He looked at us, then down the hallway. He looked at where the door used to be, then glanced back at us. I could imagine the gears turning slowly in his head, and based on the expression on his face, several of those gears were missing teeth and didn't run quite right.

"What?" I asked.

He shifted from one foot to another and back again. The classic potty dance.

"You have to go?" I asked?

He nodded.

"Well, then go."

"Daddy says I need to lock the door when I go. But Mac broke the door."

"That's not your fault that you can't do it. Go attend to your business. We'll keep a look out for you," I said. The guy next to me threw a subtle snicker, but I ignored it.

Once again, Bubba looked from the door to us to the hallway.

"Go. We'll still be here when you get back," I said.

Bubba grinned and pointed a finger at us. "Okay, but don't you move an inch. I'll be watching."

Bubba took off at a quick shuffle down the hall and I watched him start to undo his belt as he walked. The bathroom was two doors down, about twenty feet. He pushed the door open and looked back at us. "Don't you move," he hollered, then disappeared.

I heard the chair creak next to me, and when I looked over, the man was up. I reached over, grabbed his arm, and guided him back to his chair.

"Not yet," I said.

"What? No! Let's get out of here now!" he protested.

He'd barely finished speaking when the door opened. Bubba stuck his head out, noticed we were still there, and headed back in.

"How many times a day does he go?" I asked.

"I don't know, since I've never bothered to count. Eight or ten probably," the man said.

"Okay. Let's sit this one out," I said. "Wait awhile and keep an eye on what happens outside."

"I can tell you that. Eventually, they're going to move your truck. They'll either drive it or drag it, but either way, they'll clean up the mess to get ready for the next unlucky folks to pass through here."

"When will that be?" I asked.

"Hard to say. They're somewhat organized, but they're also inefficient and lazy, so it could sit there overnight. But eventually the leader will come through and want it gone."

"He said he'd come back to talk to me," I said. "When do you think that will happen?"

We both turned our heads at the same time when we heard a door open. Bubba's head appeared, and when he discovered we were both there, he returned to his business.

"He said the same thing to me but didn't return until the next day. I'm guessing he's trying to wear us down, so we'll be happy to join his little circus."

It made sense to me, but I had no intention of sticking around. I had people to see and places to be.

I lowered my voice to a bit above a whisper. "Okay, here's what I'm thinking. Bubba's going to come back after his potty break and realize we're still here. That should ease his mind a bit. He'll keep drinking, and the next time he goes, we scamper out of here, get in my truck, and hightail it out of here. Where were you headed when you ended up here?"

"Baton Rouge." The man took his glasses off and worked through the motion of cleaning them with his shirttail. "My home is there."

"You're a long way from home."

"My daughter gave birth to a boy. She lives up in Huntsville with her family. I want to move up there to be closer to the grandkids, but my wife insists we stay in Baton Rouge. She's adamant that she doesn't abandon the farm that's been in her family for three hundred years. She says since she was born there, she wants to die there."

"What do you think about that?"

He stared at his glasses for another moment, shrugged, and put them back on. "I think she's a fool to think that way. She's been in denial for a long time and expects that any day now everything will go back to normal. In the meantime, she sits out on the front porch with her papaw's shotgun, waiting to defend her birthright."

I nodded, not knowing what to say next.

"What's your story?" he asked.

"Not much. I was living in Charlotte when things turned to crap. I moved to my uncle's farm in southwestern Virginia. It's as off the grid as I can get it, and pretty remote to boot, so I think I'm good there for a long time."

"Then why are you stuck here in Alabama? That's three states away from home."

"Well, there is this girl…"

"Isn't that how all those stories develop? Something about a girl?" the man interjected.

I smiled. "Yeah, I suppose."

I sat ready to tell him the complete story, but the bathroom door creaked open, and Bubba came out. He grinned when he spotted us still sitting there.

"I told you we'd still be here when you got back. And your fly is open," I said.

Bubba looked down. His cheeks reddened, and he turned around to close the open barn door. He took a long drink from his jug of lemonade, belched, set the jug down, and wiped his mouth with the back of his hand.

"Can I have some of that?" I asked. "I'm thirsty and my head hurts. Do you have any aspirin?"

Bubba stepped in front of his jugs, as if protecting them from a bear. "Oh, no. This is my special drink. You can't have any. You can have water when it's feeding time."

"When is feeding time?"

"Soon." Bubba turned his attention to the window even though there was nothing happening outside.

"When is feeding time?" I whispered to the man next to me.

"It varies," he whispered back. "And don't expect a feast. The meal ranges in scale from canned beef stew to nothing but potatoes."

"Nice. I can't wait."

I sat back in my chair and waited. My head throbbed as I sat, but as a couple of hours passed, the pain lessened. At one point, my comrade needed to use the toilet, so Bubba escorted us both there. I waited outside in the hallway while the man did his business, and when he finished, I took my turn. Before I entered the bathroom, I had visions of a large window that led outside that I could easily open and slip through, but it turned out to be an interior room with nothing but a toilet and a sink. I forced myself to empty my bladder and checked the sink, but found no water there, even though the toilet flushed and worked fine. Briefly I thought for a moment about taking a drink from the tank, but decided in the end I wasn't that desperate. I'd keep it in mind, though.

Bubba escorted us back to our seats and returned to his post. The shadows were growing long outside, so I knew the end of the day was fast approaching. I also noticed the third of his three jugs was half empty. A few minutes later, he started his dance again.

"Go on," I said. "We'll keep an eye on the place."

Bubba had none of the hesitation he'd had earlier in the day. Without a word, he headed toward the bathroom. When the door closed behind him, I looked over at my new friend.

"You ready to get out of here?"

My buddy was on his feet before I finished the sentence. I stood, looked down the hallway to check if Bubba was there, and crept toward the door. The front door stood recessed into the building, so I stepped outside, stopped, and looked down the street in both directions.

"Is there anyone there?"

"No," I said. "Okay, here's the plan. Make a run for the truck and jump in. The passenger side door doesn't open, so you'll have to jump in the back. The door slides down from the top, so close that the second you get in there and sit down. It'll be a bumpy ride."

"Got it," he said.

I crouched, ready to run, but then I spotted a cowboy carrying a rifle approach the intersection. I backed into the doorway, waiting for the alarm that would announce that he'd spotted me, but it didn't come. Holding my breath, I counted to twenty, then peeked my head around the corner. The intersection was empty.

"Okay. Let's go. And be quiet."

I swallowed a big gulp of air, then stepped a few feet out onto the road. I wanted to stop and look around, but I determined that would do nothing for me but waste time I didn't have. It seemed like a year, but in reality, we crossed the street in ten seconds or less. I watched as he climbed into the truck's rear while I slid into the driver's seat. The key was gone from the ignition.

I didn't panic. I simply reached under the mail shelf next to the driver's seat and grabbed the magnetic key holder I'd stashed under the shelf. It took only a few seconds to extract one of the half-dozen keys I had in there and start the truck. The truck roared to life, and when I say roared, I meant it started like a combination of a jet airplane and a dump truck. I understood I had only a couple of seconds before anyone within a four-block radius heard my engine. I threw the truck into Reverse and gave it some gas. Lucky for me, I hadn't impacted the wall hard enough to crack the engine block or break an axle. Although there was a gnashing of brick on the metal as I pulled away, I managed to back up. Since going left wasn't an option, I pulled forward to the intersection I'd blindly turned around, then turned left, going the wrong way down a one-way street.

"They're coming," my new friend announced.

"Okay, hold on."

Before me there were two cars blocking the road, but not wanting to stop, I rolled up onto the sidewalk and ran over a No Parking sign. As I neared the intersection, a tall woman dressed all in denim ran out into the street and pointed a gun at me. I jerked the steering wheel, aimed for her, and pressed the gas pedal. I didn't want to run her down, but I'd had enough of being shot at for one day. Lucky for me, she stepped aside and let me pass. As I sped past her, I looked out the window and saw a manic grin on her face. Once I was by her, she stepped back into the street, leveled the gun, and pulled the trigger. I didn't detect an impact, so I guessed she'd missed the truck completely.

I drove down two blocks until I saw no one behind me, then made a left turn, keeping my foot on the gas. The road dead ended a few blocks ahead, and the tires squealed as I made another turn sharp enough I almost went up on two wheels. From the back, I caught a muted clunk.

"Sorry," I yelled.

I spotted a sign for the highway I needed, then turned another block and sped away from the city at an unsafe speed. The blocks flew by like pickets on a fence and I didn't let up until the city turned to suburbs. As my adrenaline wore off, I eased off the gas pedal and slowed down to forty miles an hour.

"Everything okay back there?" I asked.

I waited a second for an answer but didn't get one. After another few seconds, I turned my head to look behind me and saw the man's shoulder, but nothing more. Wanting a good place to pull over, I looked at the road ahead and saw a sign for a fast-food chicken place a half mile up the road. I pulled into the lot and around to the back side of the building, where no one would see us from the road. I parked the truck and went into the back. My new best friend was lying on the floor face down.

"Hey, time to wake up. We need to get going," I said.

I shook his shoulder, but he didn't budge. The first thing that ran through my mind was that when I took the hard corner, he'd lost his balance and hit his head. When I turned him over and saw his shirt front full of blood, I realized he'd taken the full brunt of the shotgun blast from the last woman we'd encountered.

"Aw, shit," I said. "Sorry, man."

I sat down next to him and put my hand on his shoulder.

"I guess it was a poor plan, after all. Maybe I should have run when I had the chance."

I looked up and saw he hadn't closed the back door like I'd requested. I realized that once he failed to do that, he'd been unprotected. A literal fish in a barrel. I sat with him for a few minutes, unsure of what to do, then I slid the back door closed and got back in the driver's seat. I pulled out of the parking lot and got back on the road, not sure what to do with his body. Within a mile, inspiration struck when I saw a large cemetery off to my left. The cemetery had a funeral home on the property, so I pulled into the cemetery and parked my truck behind the home. I found the back door was open, so I walked in and took a quick lap around the premises. The funeral home had three rooms for services, all decked out with chairs covered in black, candles at the front, and draped in a general cloak of depression. The fourth room was a showroom of sorts. On display were several coffins of various woods, linings, and additional accouterments to take the deceased to their eternal slumber in style and comfort unknown to most of the living. On one wall was a display case filled with urns, both plain and exotic for those who wished to be cremated. In a room off of the loading dock, I found what I wanted, which was a rolling cart used to transport coffins from one place to another.

I took the cart and wheeled it out to the showroom. There, I selected the most expensive coffin in the room. According to a little plastic placard in a tasteful gold frame, they made the coffin from solid mahogany, and it had an ivory velvet interior in a French fold design. It also came with golden jewel-toned accessories, a matching pillow and throw, and to seal the deal, an adjustable eternal rest bed. I didn't know what the last thing was, but I suspected it was both fancy and unnecessary. It retailed at just under eight grand, but for my buddy, sticker price wasn't an issue. I moved the cart next to the coffin, locked the wheels, and with great effort, lifted the heavy coffin to the cart, one end at a time.

I adjusted the pillow and liner and then rolled the coffin out the door and to my truck. As gentle as I could, I placed the body inside the coffin, then pushed it back into the funeral home. I pushed him into the first room I came to and set him to rest at the front of the room. On a table sat an arrangement of fake flowers, so I placed them in the coffin and closed the lid. Exhausted, muscles aching, and coming down off my adrenaline high, I collapsed into the nearest chair. I considered saying a few words but didn't. What was I to say to a man I'd known for less than a day and had gotten killed besides?

I closed my eyes and rested for a few minutes, counting down the seconds in my head. When I was ready, I got to my feet and staggered back to the truck. Once there, I took a moment to assess what I had, which wasn't much. As I suspected, the back was empty, except for the drying blood on the floor. They'd also taken my CD player, the CDs, and the batteries. Fortunately, my atlas was on the floor, except it now had a muddy boot print on the cover. The last thing I checked was my secret compartment, where I exhaled a long breath when I found everything intact.

I consulted the atlas, even though I was sure of the route, then started the engine and drove down the long driveway to the gate. I stopped and looked both ways before pulling out into the street.

One last look in my side mirror and I continued on my journey. I shuddered when I realized I'd gotten a man killed and had not even bothered to learn his name.

CHAPTER ELEVEN

There wasn't much to Coaling, Mississippi, but I didn't need much. A mile outside of town, I found a small auto repair shop and salvage yard, and I pulled in backwards in one of the bays and shut and locked the door. I wanted sleep, but before I could get that, I needed to see if I could replace some items that were stolen from me in Birmingham. Within the bay, I discovered a small green toolbox behind a workbench, and, to my surprise, it contained a nice variety of screwdrivers, wrenches, a hammer, and a small socket set. I also found a tire iron, even though my spares were gone. I figured I'd find replacements in the salvage yard, but the sun was almost gone. In the shop's office under the desk, I found a battery-powered lantern, and to my surprise, it came to life the second I pressed the button.

Also, to my surprise, I found an almost fully stocked vending machine in the waiting room. It was about half the size of the ones I'd seen in cafeterias. Even so, it had food in it. I retrieved the tire iron, found an empty cardboard box, and got to work on the vending machine. It took a few minutes to break open the cornucopia, but once I did, I got rewarded with several mini bags of potato chips and pretzels. I'd also scored two dozen candy bars and six packs of gum. I was going to live high on the hog tonight. The business didn't have a soda vending machine, but it had a mini fridge beneath the counter the coffee machine sat on. I opened the fridge and pulled from it nine bottles of water. I left the long-expired bottle of peppermint coffee creamer behind.

Finding nothing else of value in the room, I carried my box of food back to the truck and sat on the tailgate. I opened a Snickers bar and bit into it. The explosion of flavor in my mouth was immediate and welcomed. The chocolate was a treat, and although I'd never been a fan of nuts, I knew I'd get some protein from the ones in the candy. Since I'd had the large lunch a few hours before, I wasn't too hungry, so I ate only half of the bar, then folded over the open wrapper and placed it back in the box.

I yawned and leaned back to lie flat in the truck. In my head, I made a list of things I should acquire to make the trip better. A sleeping bag. Extra gas cans and hopefully a siphon. Better luck. I thought for a moment about the drying blood a few feet above my head and resolved to clean up that mess before I left in the morning. I considered finding a new windshield, but I had neither the skill nor replacement to make that happen. Sadly, I thought about abandoning my old mail truck altogether, and although the old truck and I had been through a lot over the last year, it was probably best to find one that didn't have bullet holes and a destroyed windshield. I added that to my mental list as well.

My eyes were closed, and I was on the verge of sleep when I heard a muffled beeping.

"Kayla!" I yelled as I sat straight up. I jumped from the truck and retrieved my backpack from the secret compartment. I opened the zipper and pawed around inside until I finally had the phone in hand.

"Hello? Kayla?"

"Baker? Where have you been? I've been calling for almost two hours."

I relaxed when I heard her voice.

"Kayla, I'm so sorry. I ran into some trouble today and I'm only now getting settled for the night. Where are you?"

"I'm in a little town called Delhi, Louisiana. It's about forty miles from Vicksburg. I'm going to rest here for a few hours and move on. I should be in Jackson in two or three hours after I leave here."

"Hold on, I'll be right back." I set down the phone and retrieved my atlas. After a minute, I found where I was, where she was, and compared the distances to our meeting point. "I'm back. You don't need to be in any hurry. I've got probably another half day before I will be there."

"Okay. Do you know where we should meet?" Kayla asked.

I opened the atlas to the Jackson city insert and gave it a quick look. "Do you have a map?"

"Not of Mississippi, but I'm sure I can find one somewhere."

"Okay. Good. The airport is on the east side of the city. Just south of that is a cemetery. It's at the junction of Highway 80 and Airport Road."

"You want to meet at a cemetery?" she asked.

"Yep. There's a high chance of no people being there. None that will give us trouble, anyway."

"Okay. What time?"

I did some quick math in my head for estimated travel time and added an hour to find gas. The other things on my mental list would have to wait until I met up with Kayla and we could resupply together.

"Let's say high noon. That work for you?"

"Easy as pie," Kayla said. "Do you still want to touch base at eight tomorrow morning?"

"Yeah, we probably should," I said, although I planned to be most of the way to Jackson by then.

"Okay. I'll talk to you then. Goodnight, Baker."

Kayla clicked off, and I put down the phone. I had to fight the urge to take another pass through the shop to search for supplies, but I didn't want to risk anyone seeing the light. Exhausted, I also needed sleep, so I laid down, put my head on my arm and before I knew it, I was dreaming about a special reunion and better days.

I woke the next morning to the trill of the phone. As I rose, my back protested from sleeping on the truck floor all night. The sun was streaming in through the shop windows, and I wondered how long I'd overslept.

"Kayla?" I said into the phone.

"Baker? I've got a problem."

My heart skipped a beat when I heard those words. I really didn't need any more problems or delays on this adventure.

"What is it?" I asked.

"The bridge is gone."

"What bridge?" I asked. "Can't you go around or find another?"

"The bridge over the Mississippi River," Kayla said.

I slapped my forehead. How could I have been so dumb to think that the military had taken out the bridge over the smaller rivers like the Tennessee, but somehow ignored the ones that spanned America's largest river. "Hold on, Kayla."

My trusty atlas was laying right next to me where I'd placed it last, and I picked it up and turned to Mississippi. I found where Kayla was going to cross at Vicksburg and ran my finger north and south following the river and looked for the next available crossings. It looked like it was a hundred miles in either direction.

"Kayla?"

"Yeah?"

"You're across the river from Vicksburg, right?"

"Yes."

I flipped to the Louisiana page and glanced at it. "It looks like there's a little town close to you called Delta."

"I saw a sign for that. I think it's a bit to the north."

"Okay. Go there and hunker down. I'll come to you. I'll go to Vicksburg and find a boat or barge or something to get across the river. Once I do, I'll call you when I get across the river. If I don't make it there by eight tonight, I'll call you then and give you an update. Sound good?"

She apologized for causing an inconvenience and gave me a few words of encouragement before she hung up.

I stood and stretched to get the knots out of my back, then ate the other half of my Snickers bar and nursed a bottle of water. Once I finished breakfast, I did another pass through the shop. I found four gas cans. Two were empty five-gallon cans, one was a quarter-full two-gallon can, and the last one-gallon can appeared filled to the brim. I also discovered a rudimentary siphon pump on the bottom shelf of a workbench.

I checked a few of the cars on the property and collected enough gas to fill all the gas cans. When I had all my hatches battened down, I got in my truck and pulled out of the garage.

Feeling a need for speed, I broke my rule about taking only local roads and headed for the interstate just east of Tuscaloosa to move things along faster. By faster, I meant no more than sixty. Once I pushed it to over that, the truck would shake, but I didn't want to take a delay by looking for another vehicle. Instead, I kept it at just under sixty and made slow but steady progress.

The interstate stayed relatively clear. The only issues I had were several closed off-ramps I hadn't intended to use anyway, and a large pileup on the eastern outskirts of Jackson. That one forced me to leave the interstate, take surface streets for a couple of miles, then hop back on.

A half hour west of Jackson, I decided I needed a break. The gas gauge was dipping low, and my back ached from the uncomfortable ride. I'd also been daydreaming of another Snickers and perhaps a bag of potato chips. I spotted a gas station sign in the distance and pulled off of the interstate. Once I exited the interstate, I did a U-turn and pulled into the gas station. The pumps weren't on, but I'd learned to get around that to access the underground tanks. I'd also learned that the rural stations offered much better chances of hitting pay dirt than the urban ones did.

I pulled my truck up to the tanks, pointing it outward. After I lined up my near empty gas cans, I dug out my siphon, and went through my secret process to access the gas beneath the pavement. The process had me so focused that I never noticed the person approaching me from behind.

"Mister?"

The voice surprised me, since I thought I was alone. I turned around, tripped over a gas can, and fell flat on my butt. The thought of reaching for my gun was replaced with frustration when I realized I'd once again left it in the truck, where it would do the least good if I actually needed it.

The sun was in my eyes, so I couldn't see the owner of the voice until she took another step closer and blocked the light.

"Are you okay, mister?" she asked.

"I think so," I said.

She reached out a hand to help me up, which I took, although even though I doubted she could put any actual strength behind it. Before me stood a skinny girl who couldn't have been over fifteen. She wore denim shorts and a red and blue striped T-shirt that displayed her long, light, chestnut-colored limbs. A Seattle Mariners baseball cap covered her long, shoulder length raven hair.

"Can you help me?" she asked.

I looked behind her, and from side to side, wary of her being a distraction for a larger gang wanting my property or my life. I saw no other people around, so I lowered my suspicion a notch.

"What do you need? Food? Water? A ride somewhere?" I asked.

"My daddy and brother are in trouble," she said.

"Trouble how?"

"Some rovers got them. They're tied up to a tree in town," she said as she pointed toward the south.

"No one else can help?"

She shook her head. "Everyone around here is too scared. A big gang came through about a week ago. Maybe thirty or forty men. Ran a lot of folks off. Killed a bunch, too."

"I'm sorry. There's nothing I can really do against forty men. I'm not Superman."

"There's not that many anymore. Most of them cleared out. There's only about five or six left."

"I don't know what I can do against six men," I said. "I'd probably get killed."

She frowned, which only triggered a deep-rooted feeling of guilt in me.

"Okay. I'll tell you what. I'll take a look. But if it's too dangerous or I don't think there's anything I can do, I'm going to walk away. Is that a fair deal?"

She considered it for a moment, then nodded. "Okay."

"Okay, then. Let me finish this and then I'll take you into town. Unless you've got your own car here somewhere."

She smiled and shook her head. "No."

She watched as I tinkered with the gas. After a few false starts, I got the siphon to work and started filling my cans.

"What's your name?" I asked.

"Jasmine."

"Jasmine. Pretty name. I'm Baker."

"Baker? That's a funny name," she giggled.

"No funnier than Jasmine. You think you can take this can and fill my truck?"

She nodded, and I handed her one of the cans. When she stepped away, I filled the other cans. When she returned, I gave her another can and filled up the empty one, and we continued like that until both the truck's tank and the gas cans were full.

When we finished, I helped her into the truck, wishing I'd cleaned up the blood stain. Although overnight it had dried darker, and I hoped if she noticed it she'd mistake it for rust.

Jasmine never said a word about the stain. Instead, she kneeled on the floor next to my seat and guided me toward town. As we got into the heart of the small town, I realized just how small it was. On Main Street, the tallest buildings around were only two stories, and all the shop fronts had an old-time feel to them.

"Park up by that blue building. We'll walk from there," Jasmine said.

I pulled up where she told me to and I noticed the small building, about the size of a small one-bedroom house, was the town's police department. I shut down the engine, and we left the truck.

"Holy God," I sputtered as I got out of the truck and looked at the next lot over where the town's water tower stood. It gave me a punch in the gut I wasn't expecting. The tank at the top gleamed in white paint and carried the town's name emblazoned in black, just like any other old-fashioned water tower in American. What made this one different was the naked people hanging by the neck from the crossbeams. I didn't count, but there were at least twenty of them. The majority were Black men, but I spotted one Black woman and one White man among them.

"Ain't no God here," Jasmine said dourly. "God left us a long time ago. Come on and be quiet."

After a long minute, I pulled my eyes from the corpses and followed Jasmine down a short street. We crossed over a set of railroad tracks, then walked past two mobile homes. We cut through a small copse of trees, then she slowed and crouched when we got to the far edge. I slipped in behind her and looked over her shoulder at where she was pointing.

Perhaps fifty yards away on the opposite edge of the property, I spotted two men, who I assumed to be Jasmine's father and brother, tied naked to the trunk of two apple trees. Sitting under the shade in lawn chairs were four men. One man got up, took a drink from a bottle, and passed the bottle to the person next to him. He bent down and picked something up from the ground, but from the distance I couldn't tell what it was. The man approached the smaller of the bound men and moved his arm back. The crack of the whip and the screams from Jasmine's brother hit my ears at the same time.

Jasmine backed into me, and I gave her some room and she went back in the direction we'd come. I crouched down and watched in horror. Her brother got three lashes in total. Although the sound of the whip snapping stayed constant, the screams from the boy and the laughter from the men grew louder with each beating. Satisfied, the man dropped the whip to the ground and took his seat.

I was about to leave the area when I saw the door open. A woman walked out. I assumed it was Jasmine's mother. She wore a knee-length blue skirt and nothing else. She carried a tray of what looked like sandwiches, and behind her, the fifth man followed, holding a dog leash that was connected to a collar she wore around her neck. I'd seen enough.

Silently, I stood and turned to find Jasmine. I'd made it almost as far as the mobile homes when my legs gave out. I dropped to my knees and retched.

CHAPTER TWELVE

Once I felt my composure return and my legs had turned from rubber back to muscle and bone, I stood and retraced my steps back to my truck. I found Jasmine sitting on the side of the police station, her back to the building, caught in a small patch of shade. At first, I didn't think she noticed my approach, but as I got closer, she lifted her head and looked at me. I could tell she'd been crying but had wiped away the tears before I'd arrived.

I sat down next to her. The little patch of shade was refreshing, and the wet grass seeped through the seat of my jeans, but considering what I'd seen, that didn't seem like that big of a deal.

"There's no one else?"

Jasmine shook her head.

"Everyone leave town besides you?"

She shook her head again. "Nope. In the beginning we lost about half. When the rovers got here, more left, but those who stayed hide in their houses except for when they need to find food or whatnot. They're too scared to come out otherwise."

"What about the police?" I said, rapping my knuckles on the wood siding of the building.

"The police chief was one of the men in the chairs," she answered. "He was more than happy to join up with the rovers. It was him who decided who they would make an example of. His words, not mine."

"What do you mean by example?"

Jasmine jabbed a thumb behind her. At first, I didn't realize what she meant, then I remembered the people treated like a pile of wet laundry.

"Oh."

We sat for a few minutes without speaking.

"Why are they doing this to your family?" I asked.

Jasmine shrugged. "I don't know. The chief has always had it in for my daddy. I don't know why. He was always harassing him and following him through town. Gave him a ticket once for jaywalking across Main Street. Everybody crosses Main Street like that. Everybody."

It was my turn to nod. I sat, thinking. The minutes stretched out like the highway I wished I was on right now, headed toward the Mississippi. Toward Kayla. Every fiber of my being wanted me to jump in my truck and leave this town. But I couldn't. Not after what I'd seen in the last hour.

"Jasmine, I need to be honest with you. I'm not sure if there is anything I can do. The odds are five against one. If there were others around who might help, I'd say, maybe. But on my own? I'd probably get us all killed. Think. There's no one around who could help me?"

"The only one crazy enough might be Flagman," Jasmine said.

"Who's Flagman?" I asked.

"Come on," Jasmine said, getting to her feet. I followed her to my truck.

Once inside, I fired up the engine and Jasmine directed me to the outskirts of town. She directed me down a dirt road, and a quarter of a mile later, I pulled up to a house and parked the truck. The house itself was nondescript, but what really grabbed my attention was the sheer amount of Americana going on. Six flag poles stood in the front yard. Five of the poles had the American flag blowing in the breeze, with a flag representing one of the armed services right below it. The sixth pole, the tallest, held the American flag, and below that, the state flag of Mississippi. Perched atop the roof at the corners were bald eagles, carved from wood. Red, white, and blue bunting hung under the gutters, and the doormat in front of the door proclaimed that only true Americans were welcome inside.

"Are we okay to be here?" I asked, as Jasmine guided me to the front door.

Before she could answer, the screen door squealed open, and a man stepped onto the porch. The man who stepped out towered a good five inches above me. He wore blue jeans, a T-shirt emblazoned with the American flag and house shoes. In his right hand the bald man held a .45, which looked big enough to put a hole in my belly large enough to hold a volleyball.

"Who are you?" he asked me, gesturing with the gun. "What do you want?"

He stayed so focused on me; I don't think he even noticed Jasmine. "That's Baker. He's my friend. He's gonna help me."

"With what?"

"Can we come in and I'll tell you?" Jasmine asked.

Flagman hesitated for half a minute, grunted, and backtracked into his house. We followed. Based on the outside of the house, it shouldn't have surprised me to see what I did on the inside, but I was. Flagman had decked out the entire living room in American flags. On the windowsill were bobble heads of ex-presidents. I didn't count, but I estimated he had about two-thirds in his collection. A large photograph of a bald eagle in flight was the centerpiece of one wall, and that he'd surrounded with smaller photos of the Statue of Liberty, the White House, and the Liberty Bell, among other things. The wall opposite the eagle held a large shadowbox. In the center stood a photograph of a young man in desert fatigues and surrounding that were several awards and commendations, including a purple heart.

"Sit down," Flagman ordered. He took a seat in an old gray recliner. Jasmine and I sat on the musty brown couch. "Talk."

Jasmine started us off, telling Flagman her version, and I filled in what little I had seen. Flagman sat silent and listened as we told the story.

"So, what you need from me?" he asked when we'd finished.

"I was hoping you could help. I can't go up against five men," I said.

"How long has this been going on?" Flagman asked.

"About three weeks since the rovers came and gone," Jasmine said.

I wondered how these events could have taken place, and Flagman had no inkling of them. He looked into my eyes, and I guessed he could read my thoughts.

"I don't get out much," Flagman said. He bent over and lifted his left pants leg. Underneath, I saw the prosthetic leg. "Stepped on a mine during Desert Storm. But let me tell you, as much as I hated chasing those terrorists throughout Iraq, I hate what happened to this country ten times that."

"So, you'll help?" Jasmine asked.

Flagman thought for a moment. "I wouldn't be much good in the field but consider me operational support."

Jasmine squeaked with delight, jumped from the couch, and wrapped her arms around the man. To my surprise, he embraced her as well. I noted he'd never let go of the gun.

When Flagman offered his help as operational support, I initially took that to mean as a hype man, but he surprised me when he led me into a back bedroom and showed me enough military surplus to wage war on a small island nation. Now I found myself laying on my belly in full camouflage, including black face paint, looking through the night scope of a high-powered rifle I'd fired all of five times at a Pepsi can from twenty yards away. On the fifth shot, I hit the can in the middle and Flagman and declared I was now a trained sniper. I had my doubts.

After my weapon training, the three of us sat at the kitchen table. There, Jasmine drew a rudimentary sketch of all the buildings around the area, along with the trees and a best guess of other vegetation nearby the houses. From that, Flagman developed a plan. One that I'd have to execute pretty much on my own.

For now, the plan was to stay still and observe, which I'd been doing since a half hour after sunset. Jasmine's mom, still wearing a collar and leash, had brought out food for the men at one point, then got herded back into the house. About an hour after sunset, the men set a fire in a burn barrel, then all but one disappeared into the house. Every hour, the man outside got replaced by someone else who took the watch. I'd observed the shift change three times, and each man who came out had more or less the same routine. First, they'd check to ensure Jasmine's father and brother remained secured to the tree. Sometimes they'd walk around the perimeter of the yard, sometimes they'd head right for a lawn chair and settle into it. Flagman had guessed the best way to deal with the men was one at a time since they had me outnumbered, and based on the captor's routine, I suspected he was right.

I waited.

And worried.

I'd never killed a man before. Since the end of the world, I'd seen plenty of men killed, including my ex-best friend the day before, but the deaths had never been from my hands. I'd brought up the idea of taking them into custody, but since the entire justice system had ground to a halt, it didn't seem practical. Of course, I'd also assumed that people who would hang other people from a water tower wouldn't surrender peacefully.

I waited.

Flagman had stressed patience and stealth as my greatest assets. He'd set me up with the sniper rifle, his .45, and a knife I'd only seen in movies before.

I watched as the man in the chair put his arms in the air and stretched. Then he stood and, after checking on his captives, started a lazy loop around the perimeter of the yard. At one point, he started walking toward me, and I backed up from the bush, glad that a late afternoon storm had dampened the earth enough to hide my noise as I crawled over the fallen leaves. I got to my feet and duck walked a few yards back, then froze. From there, I watched as the man stopped near the bush I'd just vacated. As I held my breath, he undid his pants and urinated.

Not wanting to risk a shot, I unsheathed the knife and waited. When he finished his business, he got himself back together and took a few steps to finish his perimeter check. I waited, and a second later, when he'd almost passed me, I stepped forward, ready to stab him in the chest. At the last second, he sensed my movement and turned toward me. He saw the knife glint in the moonlight, then thrust his arm at me to block my blow. Instead of getting him right in the ribs, his deflection caused my arm to slide up. My blade found his neck, and my inertia buried the blade deep. I got spattered with his fiery blood, and he dropped immediately to his knees, pawing at his neck. I'd let go of the knife when he fell, and his hand found it, and ripped away the knife. He splattered me a second time, then dropped the knife. His eyes found mine and I could see the fear in him. A moment later, he gurgled, then fell.

My entire body shook uncontrollably at the horror I'd just participated in, and I crashed through the bushes toward the mobile homes. There, not far from the spot where I'd vomited earlier in the day, I vomited again. Once I'd emptied my stomach, I wiped the man's blood from my face with the sleeves of my jacket. I wanted to quit, to get in my truck and go, but I realized I'd reached the point of no return. Regrettably, I'd killed a man, and I knew when his buddies found the body, they'd either go looking for who did it, or take it out on the men tied to the apple trees. I had to finish what I started.

When I returned to the scene of the crime, I found the knife and wiped the blood from it on the man's jeans before replacing it in the sheath. After I'd completed that task, I dragged the man's body back through the trees and hid it behind the remains of the downed tree.

I took up my position and looked through the scope. I saw the expanse of the yard before me, and I had a clear line of sight to the men against the trees. It was then I realized I'd made a mistake. From where I stood, if I shot at an enemy and missed, I'd hit the good guys. I knew I needed to remove them from the equation, so I followed the tree line until I'd reached the far side of the yard. I approached the apples trees from the opposite side. The older man spotted me as I slowly approached. I put my finger to my lips, and he nodded.

I got closer and whispered in his ear. "It's okay. I'm a friend of Jasmine. Can you walk?"

He smacked his lips a couple of times to moisten them, then answered. "I can try."

"I'm going to cut you guys loose. Take him back through the woods behind me."

"My wife…" he started.

"I know. I'll get her, too."

With haste, I removed the knife and cut through the ropes of both men. They were both unsteady on their feet and leaned on each other as they disappeared into the trees. When the men slipped from sight, I approached the house, careful to stay near the building. I looked in the windows, but all was dark. I took a position at the corner on the opposite end of the door. From there, I assumed that whoever came out for the next shift would notice the men were missing and go in that direction.

I waited.

When the door squealed open, the next man came out, saw his captives missing, and took a few fast steps toward the apple tree. When he stopped, I put the middle of his back in my sight and pulled the trigger. The rifle barked and a moment later the man fell forward, face first, into the tree Jasmine's brother had occupied.

The report seemed loud enough to wake the living, and I heard a muffled voice from inside the house. I lined up my rifle parallel to the house, hoping to catch the next person as they came out the door. The next man out of the house came rushing out. I fired, but he'd moved too fast, and I missed him. He turned around and started to pull a gun from his belt. But I had the advantage since I'd already lined him up in my scope. I fired, and he fell.

Three down. Two to go.

Once again, I waited, although my body chemistry had jacked me up, and I wanted to run into the house with guns blazing to finish the deed. Instead, I forced myself to hold still.

I expected the fourth man to rush from the house, but he didn't. Instead, I detected some clunking on the inside of the building, as if furniture was being overturned, then things went silent.

Several minutes later, a window in front of me silently slid open and the muzzle from a shotgun inched out and swept the area. I leaned my rifle against the house and drew the handgun from its holster. I crept to the window and positioned myself under it. The gun above me moved from right above my head to the left. There, it stopped for a moment, then came back the other way. When it got back above me, it paused again. With my left hand, I grabbed the gun and jerked it forward. As I did, I raised my .45 and fired two quick shots into the open window. The shotgun fell and landed in the grass, and a second later, an arm poked out the window, then stopped moving.

"Fuck!" I heard from inside the house.

I retreated to the corner and retrieved the rifle.

Then I waited. Nothing happened for a good long while. I moved closer to the open window.

"Come out. We've got the house surrounded," I yelled.

"Bullshit!" came the response.

"I've got ten men with flash-bang grenades waiting for my order to enter. If you don't come out, we're coming in," I screamed. "You've got to the count of ten."

"You'll kill the woman," the man yelled back.

"We've already saved the other two. We'll take the chance. You're down to a count of five."

Silence descended, and I waited.

A woman shrieked. "I'm coming out," the man said.

I moved halfway down the house, closer to the door, and trained my rifle on the spot. The door creaked and out stepped the woman, and on her back like a second skin was the last man standing. He forced her down the stairs and into the yard. Looking through the scope, I saw I didn't have a good shot. Shooting a man at center mass was hard enough, but I didn't have the skill to fire a shot and hit the man without killing her as well. I needed a better opportunity.

I waited.

The couple moved as one. A step into the yard, and then another. I wasn't sure what his plan was, since there was nowhere to go.

"That's far enough," I said. "Let her go and we'll let you go."

The man pivoted, so the woman was directly in my sight line. "If you shoot, you'll kill her."

"And my men will kill you," I said.

The man looked around, then laughed. "There's no one here. New plan. I'll shoot you instead."

Too late, I realized I'd made a mistake. I should have stayed at the corner of the house to take cover. Once again, I'd let someone get the drop on me.

"Drop the gun," the man said.

Instead of simply dropping the gun, I tossed the rifle forward toward the man. He took a step backward to avoid getting hit by it, and when he did, Jasmine's father hit the man on the side of the head with a shovel. The man fell to the earth, and Jasmine's father took a moment to spit on him.

For a moment, I wondered what was next, and before I could say a word to the man, my world went dark.

Birds. I heard birds. Once I opened my eyes, I looked to my right and saw two robins searching for breakfast. I moaned and sat up. Although I was still on the ground, there was a pillow under my head and a blanket covering me. In front of me, Jasmine was curled up in a lawn chair, also covered in a blanket.

"What happened?" I asked.

"You passed out," Jasmine said. "Daddy said it was the darnedest thing he ever saw. You came all up in here like Clint Eastwood, took out the bad buys, and passed out. They tried to get you inside, but nobody had the strength to get you up."

I struggled to my feet and stretched. There was a knot in the small of my back that would take forever to work out. I looked around the yard. The two men I'd shot still lay where they fell. I noticed the arm was missing from the window, so I assumed that someone had moved the body. They'd also trussed the last captor like a Thanksgiving turkey. Someone had covered his head with a pillowcase, so I couldn't tell what his condition was.

I heard a noise behind me, and I turned and saw a dozen people walking up a stone driveway I hadn't noticed before. In the lead was a man I recognized as Jasmine's dad. He changed direction and walked toward me. I put out a hand for a shake, but he gathered me into a hug instead. When he finally let me go, he had tears in his eyes.

"Thank you," he said.

"Are your wife and son okay?" I asked.

He nodded. "Because of you."

As we stood together in the awkwardness, I saw a few men enter the house, and a few more gathered up the bodies outside. Two men got the remaining captor to his feet and started leading him down the driveway. I didn't want to know what the future held for him.

"Can you stay?" Jasmine's father asked.

I shook my head. "No. I've got to get going. I have another friend who needs my help."

He nodded, then hugged me again. "If you ever come back this way, you stop in. You're always welcome here, son."

I patted him on the back, and he let me go and plodded toward the house.

"Flagman says he wants his weapons back. You can keep the clothes, though," Jasmine said as she left her chair.

I looked around and spotted the rifle a few feet away, lying in the grass. I retrieved it and leaned it against her chair, then I added the .45 and the knife to the pile.

"It seems you were the right man to ask for help," Jasmine said.

"I reckon so."

She rushed forward, wrapped her arms around me, and kissed my cheek.

"Baker's still a silly name," she said.

"No worse than Jasmine," I answered.

CHAPTER THIRTEEN

When I returned to my truck, still ironically parked next to the police station, I opened the back door and sat on the tailgate. I stripped off the jacket and the long-sleeved camouflage shirt that Flagman had given me and tossed them without regard into the truck. The jacket, I'd noticed, appeared crusted with blood, and it would stay that way until I found a river to soak it in. I wouldn't put it on again in its current condition. Next, I kicked off the black leather boots and tossed those in. I doubted I'd wear those again. They were a half-size too small, and my feet ached from the few brief hours I'd had them on. Lastly, I removed the camo pants and threw them onto the growing pile inside. The pants I liked since they had a good number of pockets and seemed comfortable enough, but like the jacket, they needed a good wash since I had gotten mud and blood on them.

I sat on the tailgate in my underwear and opened the half-liter bottle of water Jasmine had given me before I left and had a long drink. Once again, I got the urge to get back on the road, but I needed a little recovery time. I needed to collect my thoughts, get a hold of my feelings, and since my pulse hadn't stopped racing since the night before, I needed to calm down before I rushed headfirst into a situation I couldn't get out of.

As I drank, I looked down at my legs. I had a deep tan on my legs from where the bottom of my favorite shorts normally ended to where the top of my socks sat. On my right thigh, I spotted a tick. It wasn't moving, so I assumed it had attached. It relieved me to realize it hadn't engorged itself yet, so it couldn't have bitten me too long ago. From behind, I grabbed it as close to the skin as I dared and gently pulled until it released. The trick was to apply enough pressure to get it to let go without either leaving the tick head embedded, or even worse, having the tick get irritated enough to regurgitate into the wound. Lucky for me, the tick let go easily, and then I had to decide what to do with it. I always thought fire, acid, or lava were good ways to dispose of a tick, but since I had none of those readily available, I flicked it into the road and hoped a bird or opossum would wander by and make a snack of it.

The tick brought Jenny to mind. Jenny was one of those people who walked into my life by luck and circumstance and stayed there. If used car salesmen were the dregs of society, Jenny was the pinnacle. She was wicked smart, funny, compassionate. It's like nature took all the best qualities that a person had and combined them into one woman. Jenny's bright blue eyes never failed to sparkle, and she was a beacon of positivity and hope. She celebrated half-birthdays and was quick with a smile and a kind word. If superheroes existed in the real world, Jenny, for sure, would have been one. However, fate had other things in store for Jenny, and a tick bite gave her Lyme disease, which, in turn, led to other health complications. The lack of medical science and a glut of misinformation only hastened her struggles, and at the tender age of forty-two, Jenny's light faded out. When I received the news of her passing, I felt empty, and angry, and sad that I hadn't spoken to her in so long. But I can ensure she lives on if I can remember those qualities that endeared her to everyone she met. I could be a much better person if I worked to be a little more like Jenny and a little less like me.

Then, as if Mother Nature had read my thoughts, a robin landed on the blacktop, picked the tick from the ground, swallowed it down, and flew away. Good riddance to bad insects.

I took a moment to do a spot check for more of the little bastards, but I didn't spot any. I ran my fingers through my hair, and again, didn't come across additional ticks. Relief came over me as I sat back down and returned to the bottled water. I took a few more sips, closed the bottle, and set it aside. I stood and stretched, and as I did, I noticed a woman walk by. Before her, she pushed a shopping cart filled to the top with what looked like white bed sheets. As she moved, one wheel squeaked in protest, then spun around and squeaked again. Our eyes met, and she didn't react when she saw a white man standing in his underwear. Her face seemed stoic, chiseled from granite. Suddenly, it dawned on me where she headed, and I stepped a few paces away from the truck and looked in the direction she walked. The water tower came into view, and there I spotted four men beginning to erect ladders and makeshift scaffolding to reach the bodies.

When I got back to the truck, I shook out the camo pants and shirt and put them back on. I'd just about finished slipping into my own shoes when my phone rang.

"Hello? Kayla?"

"Baker? Are you doing okay?" she asked. I'd called her the night before and told her I'd have a night's delay, but I didn't provide any details.

"Yeah, I'm fine," I lied.

"How far out are you?" she asked.

I didn't have to guess. During a quick conversation, I'd asked Jasmine's dad how far away the Mississippi River was if I stayed on the interstate, which I fully intended to do. "I'm about a half hour from Vicksburg. Then I'll have to find a way across the river."

"So, when do you think you'll be here?"

"I've got one other thing I need to do, so I should be there in three or four hours. I'll call you the second I'm across the river, okay?"

"Yeah, fine."

"Are you okay?" I asked

"I'm fine. A woman caught me sneaking into her barn last night. By gunpoint she insisted I go with her into the main house where she fed me and put me up in her guest bedroom."

"Sounds horrible," I said after I gave her a laugh I hoped didn't sound too forced.

"Oh, it was. She practically stuffed me to death with cherry pie. I'll be fine here until you arrive."

"Good," I said. At least one of us had it easy.

"Baker?"

"Yeah?"

"Are you sure you're okay?"

I paused, caught between wanting to tell her the truth and wanting to end the conversation. "Hey, I'll talk to you in a few hours. I have to go do something. Bye, Kayla."

I disconnected the call, feeling guilty for making it so abrupt, but I needed to move. To help. I wasn't in the mood for small talk, or any other kind of talk, for that matter. Gently I put the phone down, then stared at it for a moment, wondering if I should call her back and apologize for being rude. I didn't. After I finished dressing, I closed up and locked the truck, then walked around the police station. Before me, the men had removed the first body and laid it on a bedsheet and the stoic woman was bundling it with care. She looked at me as I approached, and neither one of us spoke as I crouched to help her.

Three hours later, I was hot and sweaty as I stripped off the clothes for the second time that morning and tossed them in the truck. I drank from the bottle and resisted the urge to dump the precious commodity over my head to cool off. That luxury would need to wait until I reached the river. Once I dressed into my own clothes, I made sure everything was in place, started the truck and finally drove out of town. The second my wheels touched the interstate, I jammed the accelerator to the floor and shot down the highway like a missile.

The directions I got from Jasmine's dad were spot on, and within twenty-five minutes, I passed into the town of Vicksburg. I stayed on the interstate and took it as far as I could. White and orange construction barrels blocked the road, but even if I moved them, I wouldn't make it across the river since they'd destroyed the road. Next to the interstate bridge was a rail bridge with pedestrian access that I easily could have walked across if I could jump across the missing forty-foot section.

After I turned around, I flipped a mental coin and turned north. I passed a casino that resembled a riverboat, so I pulled into the lot and found a parking spot right by the river. I got out of the van, walked to the rail, and looked out at the mighty Mississippi. From where I stood, there was a good twenty-foot drop of sheer bedrock to the river's level, but even if I got down there, I spotted no way to get across unless I swam.

I returned to the truck and headed further north. Another mile up the road, I got lucky and spotted a marine resupply shop. I pulled into the parking lot and noticed right away a concrete ramp leading down to a pier. I traveled only halfway down when I noticed a small craft hidden by a brown tarp. Excited, I ran the rest of the way and threw the tarp back. There, bobbing in the water, was the most beautiful boat I'd ever seen. Granted, it was only a ten-foot, all-purpose Jon boat, but it had a motor attached to the back. It wouldn't be a comfortable ride, but it would get me across the river and back, provided there was enough gas. I checked the tank and knew there would be enough for the trip. I thought about shoving off right away, but I ran back to the truck and from it extracted my go bag and guns from the secret compartment and shoved the phone into the bag as well.

Once I reached the boat, I threw my pack in and set my rifle on the floor, then went to work untying the vessel from the dock. I did, then caught another lucky break when I saw the engine was an old-fashioned pull-start rather than one of the newer models that required a key. I reached back into my memory from when I went fishing with my uncle and fired it up forthwith. Although I expected some difficulty with it because my uncle's motor was always temperamental, this one started on the second pull. I adjusted the tiller, then started my way across the river.

I'd made it perhaps thirty yards when I heard voices shouting behind me. When I glanced back, I saw three men at the end of the pier screaming at me. Over the din of the engine, I couldn't quite make out the words, but based on the flailing arms and angry faces, I could tell they wanted me to return.

"Sorry. I'll be back." I yelled behind me, then returned my attention to the river in front of me. The river ran wild, and the swells were such that I didn't want to go too fast for fear that the unsteady boat would capsize.

In my periphery, I saw a small splash of water.

"Oh, shit," I said as I turned my head. Yep. The boys on the pier were now using me for target practice. I didn't understand the logic in that, since if they hit me, they'd never get their boat back. It would float with the current all the way to the gulf unless it got caught up on something. I heard the sound of metal on metal and saw a small hole an inch below the gunwale.

In a panic, I opened up the throttle and steered the craft from side to side, but since the splashes of water only got closer, I assumed that maneuver only worked in the movies. I abandoned that idea, gave the motor a little more gas, and picked an angle that sharply veered away from the men the quickest. When I caught a swell, the boat lifted temporarily from the water, and I thought my tail bone broke when I landed hard in the seat. Going too fast, I dialed it back a little to remain in control, and crouched over, hoping to make a smaller target. I didn't bother looking behind me and stayed focused on the growing horizon before me.

When I estimated I'd made it halfway across, I looked behind me and saw the men were gone from the pier.

I followed the river north, looking for a place to set in, but like the other side, I spotted bluffs too high for me to climb freehand. The river curved around to the west, and I spotted a small branch that curled around a small island before it rejoined the main river. I followed the branch, and my luck continued when I spotted a small ramp a few hundred yards ahead. I made for it, and a few minutes later, I made a hard landing, scraping the bottom of the boat on the concrete ramp under the water. After I made my way to the bow, I jumped out, then pulled the boat up the ramp until it was three-quarters of the way out of the water. I hoped it was far enough to not get taken by a rising tide, but since I had neither a trailer nor enough rope to tie it off somewhere, it had to do. From the boat, I grabbed my backpack and rifle.

The ramp led to a road, nothing more than two tire tracks that led away from the river. Having no other choice, I followed them for a quarter mile until I came to an actual road, then I turned right, away from the river, and walked on. Trees surrounded either side of the road, but a half mile later, the trees opened up. Ahead of me and to my right looked to be farmland that stretched as far as I could see. Another half mile to my left, however, stood the makings of a small town.

At a snail's pace, I walked into town. When I came to a stop sign, bleached from red to pink by heat, sun, and time, I stopped, removed the pack from my aching shoulders, and dug out the phone. I pressed the only speed dial button I had programmed in, and Kayla answered on the second ring.

"Where are you?" she asked.

I told her based on the road markers attached to the stop sign. There was a brief pause as she asked her hostess where I was in relation to them.

"Okay," she said, "go another two blocks, turn right, and walk another three blocks. I'm at the yellow house on the right. It's the only non-mobile home on the block. You can't miss it."

We said our goodbyes, and I continued on my journey. The blocks weren't large, New York City length blocks. They spanned only a hundred yards a piece, so I made quick time through town. I felt exposed being so out in the open, but I never encountered a soul as I walked. Except for one man peering out at me from a window, I saw no one at all.

No thoughts ran through my head as I plodded on, following the directions Kayla had given me. Ahead of me I spotted a water tower, and I shuddered at the sight, even though they'd painted this one in a pretty robin's egg blue and there were no people dangling from it. The sight still caused me to stop in my tracks. When my eyes dropped from the tower closer to the ground, I saw the one-story yellow house, and as I walked closer, I noticed someone sitting on the front porch. I stepped over a culvert filled with tall grass and approached the house, slipping the pack from my shoulders.

Kayla stood. She looked just as I pictured her each time I talked to her. Her blond hair looked longer than I remembered her wearing it, but her emerald green eyes held the same brightness they always did. Kayla smiled sweetly.

"Hey, there," she said, adding the extra touch of Texas twang she knew I had always gotten a kick out of.

I honestly didn't know what to say. My tears welled, and whether they were tears of joy, relief, or thankfulness, I didn't know. It didn't matter. I took another step forward, opened my arms, and she moved into my embrace, right where she belonged.

CHAPTER FOURTEEN

When we finished our hug, Kayla led me into the house. I dropped my backpack inside the front door and leaned my rifle against a bookcase. She reached for my hand and ushered me into the kitchen. The smell of the fresh pie hit me before I stepped into the room, and I got instantly transported to the before times when a person would step into a bakery and order whatever they wanted whenever they wanted. Add fresh baked goods to the list of things the human species took for granted.

"Baker, this is Mrs. Parsons."

When Kayla mentioned a woman had caught her while sneaking into a barn, in my head I pictured someone about our age. Mrs. Parsons looked beyond our age by a good forty years. She was a wisp of a woman, thin, frail, with a shock of white hair on her head and a set of light brown eyes surrounded by crow's feet.

"Ma'am," I said. "Thank you for taking care of Kayla until I got here."

Mrs. Parsons got to her feet, approached me, and gave me a hug. She came up to chest height on me, and I gave her a slight squeeze that I hoped implied my reciprocation without crushing her.

"Oh, it's been no trouble at all. Kayla is a dear. A lovely dear, I tell you. She's been a big help to me around the house while we've been waiting for you to arrive."

I glanced at Kayla, who was grinning at me and trying not to laugh. I let Mrs. Parsons escape from my grasp, and she returned to her spot at the table. As she got comfortable, I noticed she had a shotgun within reach that looked to be two-thirds her height.

"Are you ready to go?" I asked Kayla.

"Go? You can't go," Mrs. Parsons protested, rising from her chair. "I've got a pie in the oven. Kayla said you love pies. It's apple, and I even put the fancy lattice work on top."

My eyes returned to Kayla, who gave me a shrug.

"Okay," I said. "I guess we can wait for the pie. It sounds delicious."

Kayla nodded. "I know he doesn't sound enthusiastic about it. He really does love pie. Baker, can you come and take a look at my bike in the barn? I've been having problems with it."

I wanted to protest since I had little experience with bikes, but Mrs. Parsons shooed me from the kitchen before I could.

Kayla grabbed my arm and led me out the front door and around the side of the house. Although she'd mentioned a barn, the building was more like a large shed that someone would house an RV in. The building had a large garage-type door, but she guided me to a regular door on the building's side. We stepped in and Kayla flipped on the lights. I half expected to spot an RV, but the shed served mainly as a storage unit for unwanted furniture and stacks and stacks of plastic bins, which probably contained the collected treasures of an entire lifetime.

"It's over here," Kayla said.

I turned, assuming Kayla had a ten-speed, but instead I spotted a bright orange scooter. It looked scuffed up and was missing a mirror, but other than that, it seemed reliable.

"Did you ride this thing all the way from Texas?" I asked.

"No. I had to walk the first few miles. I found this in the first town I came to."

"Why walk? Why not take a car?"

"I didn't want to be seen. There were lots of people coming in and staying. I left at night and walked through people's yards and fields until I got farther north, where there was no one around."

I nodded. "Start it up. Let's see what's wrong with it."

Kayla sat on the machine and pushed the button to get it going. The engine started but emitted a high-pitched sound.

"Okay, shut it off," I said.

She did.

"How long has it made that sound?" I asked.

Kayla shrugged. "The last twenty miles or so. Can you fix it?"

I looked around for a rag, found one, and removed the scooter's oil dipstick. Since it was bone dry, there was no need to wipe it off. After I returned it to the slot, I shook my head. "I think the engine's seizing up. I can't fix it here, but if you're partial to a scooter, I'm sure I can find you one when we get back to Virginia."

Kayla frowned.

"We would have had problems getting it on the boat, anyway."

Kayla turned off the light, and we walked back to the house. Rather than go in, she sat down on the front stoop, and I joined her. For the longest time, we sat in silence, staring out at the yard.

"Are you okay?" I asked.

She sighed deeply. "I think so. I'm tired, though. Baker, I'm not kidding when I say I want to sleep for a year. It's been hard not being able to feel safe enough to sleep, you know?"

I understood. Being away from home, especially on this particular trip meant catnaps whenever I might steal them, and even settling in for the night meant sleeping with one eye open. I couldn't wait to get back to my bed, where I knew I was safe and secure.

"As least it's been an easy trip for me," she said. "Biggest problem I had was getting gas for the scooter. Sounds like you ran into some trouble, though."

I paused. "Yep."

"Want to talk about it?"

"Nope."

"Okay."

She let it drop. That was one thing I always loved about Kayla. If I didn't want to talk about something, she never pushed and would wait until I wanted or needed the discussion. Of course, I gave her the same consideration as well when there were things on her mind that she didn't want to share. We sat, neither one of us speaking for another long minute.

"So, what's the plan?" Kayla asked, snapping back from wherever she'd gone in her mind.

"Take the boat across the river. I have my truck waiting on the other side. We take a nice, leisurely ride back to Virginia." I stretched my legs out and folded one ankle over the other, trying to make it sound simpler and more casual than it had been.

Hopefully, I'd used up all my bad luck on the way down, and the way back would be much easier.

"When are we leaving?" she asked. "Are you in any hurry to get back?"

"Why? Did you want to stop off and see the sights along the way? Check out a couple of tourist traps? See Graceland?"

She playfully hit my leg. "No. I'm simply tired. Until I got here, I haven't been sleeping all that great. It's been hard trying to get comfortable and manage plenty of rest when I'm hiding out in some random barn or shed."

I nodded to show I empathized. At least I had my truck I got to stretch out in the back of when I needed a rest.

"I'd like to get back to the farm, but we can take it at an easy pace," I said. "I left Pops in charge, and although I'm sure he has things covered, it's a lot of work for him."

"Pops?" Kayla asked.

"He's my neighbor who lives up the mountain. We've been working together since I came to the farm."

I caught the screech of the screen door behind us and looked over my shoulder to where Mrs. Parsons was gesturing for us to come in. We did and settled around the kitchen table. Mrs. Parsons put the pie on the table and made a show of slicing off three generous portions and placing them on real china plates with a decorative border of light pink roses.

"This set has been in my family for over a hundred years. Can you believe it?" Mrs. Parsons said.

"No," I said. "It's in great condition."

Her face transformed into a scowl. "That's because they never used it. I remember my grandmother would bring it out for special occasions only, like Christmas dinner or Thanksgiving. But once the dinner was done, it went right back into the cabinet to wait for the next special occasion. When it got passed down to my mama, she did the same thing. Never used it but once or twice a year. When I was a child, I thought it was magical dinnerware, like it had some secret power, so they would only bring it out occasionally. Now, I think it's stupid. I can't imagine all the china sitting around, unused, because it's supposed to be special. It's only a plate."

I didn't know how to respond, but inside, I guessed she was right. My mom had a set almost like it. I took a moment to wonder what happened to that old dinnerware set, complete with a turkey platter and a gravy boat.

"You're not eating," Mrs. Parsons said, pointing her fork at me.

"Sorry. Lost in thought for a moment. This smells delicious."

It did. The combination of fresh apples and cinnamon, and something else I couldn't quite identify. I positioned my fork and sliced off the corner tip, jabbed the pie with the fork, and brought it to my lips. I hesitated for just a moment, savoring the scent before I dropped it into my mouth and began chewing.

My eyes grew wide, and I nodded, and I made an extended audible noise to exclaim how much I enjoyed the baked delight. Across the table, Mrs. Parsons put her fork down, clapped twice, and laughed.

"Oh, I knew you'd love it. Everyone around here says I've always made the best pies!"

As my outward appearance showed how much I liked the pie, internally, I stayed focused on not spitting it out. The apples were underdone and crunchy, and the bottom crust had a consistency of plumber's putty. No matter how much I chewed, I couldn't swallow it down. I felt a piece get stuck in my upper esophagus, and my eyes started to water when I realized I was mere moments away from coughing and expelling the pie all over the nice plastic tablecloth.

The tickling sensation grew worse, and I was about to lose it when I heard a knocking.

"I think there's someone at the front door, Mrs. Parsons," Kayla said.

"Who could that be?" Mrs. Parsons said. She put her napkin on the table and rose.

The second Mrs. Parsons left the kitchen, Kayla jumped to her feet, and grabbed my plate and hers.

"Spit," she ordered.

I did.

"Get rid of this while I distract her. Ditch mine, too."

As Kayla left the room, I grabbed my plate, then hers, and looked around for a place to toss them. I spotted a trash can and realized that would be too obvious. A breeze blew in through the kitchen window, and I looked to my left and spotted the curtain. I rushed to the window, opened the screen, scraped the contents of both plates onto the lawn below. When they were clean, I set the dishes on the counter and closed the screen. I listened to the footsteps on the wood floor and realized I'd get caught in a second. In the sink was a plastic basin filled with water and the few items Mrs. Parsons had dirtied making the pies. I took a breath, then just as natural as could be, I picked up the plates and forks and gently set them into the basin.

"Oh, you don't have to clean up," Mrs. Parsons said as she took her seat and picked up her fork.

"It was no trouble, ma'am, and the least I could do, considering you passed through all the trouble to make that pie."

"Would you like more?" Mrs. Parsons asked.

Kayla jumped in. "No, thank you, Mrs. Parsons. Baker says we need to leave so we can get back across the river before dark."

I smiled and nodded, then made my way to the living room. I grabbed my backpack, slipped out the door and waited on the porch for Kayla. She appeared a few minutes later, and without speaking, we headed toward the boat. When we got there, we put our backpacks into the craft, and Kayla helped me push it into the river. While she got settled, I held onto the line, and then boarded and made my way to the stern.

The engine fired up right away, and I backed us away from the bank and headed into the channel leading to the river.

"How long will it take to get across?" Kayla asked.

"Not long. Fifteen minutes." I answered.

The wind picked up, and Kayla put her hand over her head to keep her long blond locks from drifting into her face. I pointed the boat so we traveled downstream at an angle, letting the current help us along. When we reached the halfway point, Kayla raised an arm and pointed across the river.

"What's that?" she shouted to be picked up over the wind and drone of the outboard.

I looked in the direction she pointed and a terrible reaction bubbled into my stomach, and it wasn't from the pie. "Not sure."

I knew exactly what it was, but I steered the boat in that direction anyway, knowing exactly where the column of lazy black smoke originated. As we got closer to shore, the smoke grew blacker, and when we were a couple of hundred yards out, my worry got confirmed when I saw my beloved mail truck being consumed by fire.

"What's that?" Kayla asked.

"Our ride."

Before anything else could happen, my eyes caught movement as two men laying prone on the dock shifted and I saw they both had rifles.

"Kayla, get down!" I screamed as the first shot put a hole in the gunwale not more than an inch from Kayla's knee.

"Hold on!"

I swung the boat around, pointed it downstream, and opened the throttle. Another shot impacted the boat, but I knew at least Kayla was safe as long as it was my body between her and the gunmen. Another shot hit, and I looked back to see how much farther I needed to go to get out of range.

"Baker! Watch out!" Kayla screamed.

I swung my head back around just in time to spot the floating telephone pole I was about to hit. Unable to react in time, the boat hit the debris and went skyward. I expected us to tip over, but we hit the river flat on the other side, jarring me enough that I let go of the tiller. The tiller turned hard to port, and the boat swung again, threatening to capsize us. I turned and grabbed for the tiller, banging my knee on the outboard in the process. I wanted to ease it back around, but the river fought me for it, causing me to give it a jerk. The tiller turned and the boat over-corrected. I heard a scream and turned around just in time to see Kayla in the river, moving downstream with the current.

"Aw, shit! Kayla, I'm coming!" I screamed, knowing she'd never hear me. I watched her the best I could, but now and then she'd drop under the water completely and my heart would stop until she surfaced again. In an attempt to catch her, I pointed the boat downstream and at a slight angle, and opened the throttle as far as it would go.

I steered closer, then overtook her. I swung the boat around until I was sideways to the river and killed the engine. Unsteadily, I kneeled in the center of the boat, then leaned over the edge. I watched as Kayla drifted closer, her eyes wide with terror. Against common sense, I leaned over farther, my entire upper body almost in the water. I intended to grab her so she wouldn't slam into the side of the boat. A foot before she got to me, Kayla disappeared under the water again.

I stretched out farther. The river water touched the top of my head, and I fully expected to drop into the river myself. My arms flailed, then contacted something. At first, I suspected it was a branch, but then I felt Kayla's hand close around my arm. I reached with my other hand, found her arm, then backed from the water. Her arm appeared, and then her head. I pulled her to me and draped her arms over the gunwale.

"Hey, I'm going to boost you out of there, okay?" I asked.

Kayla spit out a mouthful of river water and nodded.

I reached over and grabbed her belt, counted to three, and hauled her in. I fell backward, hitting my head on the opposite gunwale, and Kayla landed on top of me, knocking the air from my lungs. My head ached, and I closed my eyes. I saw stars for a moment, and when I opened my eyes, I saw Kayla's green eyes staring into mine.

"Hi," I said.

"Can we get off of his damn river now, Huckleberry?" Kayla asked. She smiled, then pushed away from me. Once she took her seat, I got myself back together and took my seat at the outboard.

"Excellent idea," I said.

CHAPTER FIFTEEN

Once I got Kayla back in the boat and secure, I grabbed the tiller and pointed us toward the riverbank. The water moved swiftly and based on the amount of debris in the water, I suspected that there must be a powerful storm going on somewhere to the north. It wasn't long before we passed the riverboat casino, and what used to be the bridges running from Mississippi to Louisiana. Another hundred yards down the river, I eyed a spot where the erosion had cut a small inlet, and I pointed the boat in that direction and a few moments later, the boat ran aground.

Before us was a steep pile of shale that ascended for thirty yards before it turned to the steep tree-lined bank.

"Do you think you can make it up that little hill?" I asked.

Kayla looked where I pointed. Based on the difficulty she was having catching her breath, I probably shouldn't have asked.

"Do we have another option?" she asked.

"Sure. We can get back on the river and find a better place to land. The downside is, I don't know how far that would be, and if we can't find transportation, we'd have to walk that much farther to get back this way. I'm not gonna lie. Neither option is a good one."

Kayla's eyes followed the slope, and she looked downriver. "I guess I'll choose the climb. There's no way I want to go for another swim."

I nodded. "Okay, let's get on with it."

Kayla jumped out of the boat and grabbed our backpacks while I shut down the motor and pulled it from the water. We wouldn't require the boat anymore, but I guessed someone in need would come along and be grateful for the find.

I put on my backpack, picked up my rifle, and pondered the climb. I didn't know how I would do it one-handed, so I removed the backpack and shoved the rifle as far into it as I could. When I put the backpack on again, the rifle extended a good two feet above my head, so I made a mental note to try to stay as low as I could once I got to the trees.

"Are you ready?" I asked.

Kayla responded by taking a last look at the hill and began the climb without saying a word. I hung back for a few seconds and watched her as she carefully plotted each step as she climbed, instinctively picking out the best route as she ascended the hill. She stopped, turned around, and spotted me watching her.

"You coming?" she asked.

I grinned like an idiot, then started my climb, trying to mimic the route she took. Above me, Kayla scampered up the shale like a mountain goat. I had a more arduous climb, slipping every third step I took and envisioning myself rolling down to the river and breaking my neck when I hit the bottom. I paid so much attention to where I placed my feet that I got startled when Kayla's hand popped into my visual field. When I looked up, I saw she'd made it to the tree line, and she held onto a branch while offering her other hand to me. I took it, and she gave me the boost I needed to make it the last couple of feet.

"You okay?" she asked.

"Yeah. That was tougher than I assumed it would be."

She looked at the route ahead. "It will be easier going from here. We can use the tree branches to help pull us up. I think another two hundred yards or so, and we'll be back on level ground."

"This seems to be easy for you," I said.

Kayla shrugged. "It's actually not too bad. I love hiking and spent some time out in the Rockies. Granted, a lot of those trails the park groomed, but the experience helped."

"Okay, then, you're in charge. Get us out of here," I said.

Kayla took a moment to plot her course, gave me an encouraging word, then took off. I waited until she was a few feet ahead of me and then followed her, paying close attention to every step she took and every tree she used for support.

By the time I'd reached the third tree, I realized the rifle in the backpack idea wouldn't work since it kept getting caught on branches. I stopped for a moment, removed the gun, and tucked it under my arm. It would impede my progress, but I didn't want to leave it behind.

As I continued the climb, my legs began to cramp, and my back ached. When I thought I couldn't go any more, I looked up and saw Kayla a good twenty yards ahead, waiting for me.

"You're almost there, Baker. One more push and you're at the top."

I felt like crying, and I still wanted to stop, but I pushed on, and a few minutes later, I hit the apex. Trees still surrounded us, but the terrain was nice and flat. Twenty feet away, I spotted a tree stump and made a beeline for it. When I got there, I sat and shrugged off the backpack and set it on the ground with the rifle. I took off my hat and dropped that as well. Sweat poured down my face, so I pulled my shirt loose and wiped my face with it. Kayla held out a water bottle, and I took it and drank a bit, careful not to overindulge.

"That was a worse idea than I originally thought," I said, handing the bottle back to Kayla.

"Well, we could go back down and take the boat to a better landing spot," Kayla said.

I wanted to argue with her, but she threw me a sweet smile and I let it drop. Self-reflection is important, and I realized that my current state of exhaustion made me edgy.

"Where to next?" I asked.

Kayla shrugged, then pointed. "That way? If we keep going away from the river, we're bound to hit a road. Eventually."

"Sounds like a logical plan to me. Let's go," I said. With a grunt, I stood, tucked my shirt back in, and picked up my backpack and rifle.

Kayla went ahead, picking our way through the trees, and it surprised and delighted me when we walked only sixty feet, then left the trees and entered someone's backyard. Not wanting trouble, we followed the trees along the perimeter of the property, and then followed the driveway until we came to a paved road.

"Should we go left, or right?" Kayla asked when our feet hit the concrete.

From the pocket of my backpack, I found and consulted my compass. I knew Vicksburg stood to the north of us, and the red needle pointed left, so we started in that direction. We walked for only a half mile when we spotted a hotel, a burned-down restaurant, and a sign pointing to the on-ramp of the interstate.

We walked up the ramp and strolled on the interstate until we got to the first off-ramp we came to. Looking down the intersecting road, we spotted a handful of restaurants, a big box store, an auto body shop, and a car dealership. Preferring to drive rather than walk, we headed to the dealership first. Although there were plenty of cars on the lot, we struck out when we couldn't find a single key to any of them. Next, we headed to the auto body shop. There, we found plenty of keys to vehicles, but not a single car on the property was in working order.

"I don't really relish walking all the way back to Virginia," I said as we put the dealership behind us and headed back to the interstate.

"Let's try over there," Kayla said.

She led me across the street, then down the road to where a large, big box store sat. Like most stores I'd encountered, the doors hung askew, and we walked right in. Kayla, ever the optimist, grabbed a cart.

"Let's go shopping," she said as we walked deeper into the store.

I considered pulling my flashlight out of the backpack, but as we wandered deeper into the store, I noticed the skylights overhead and figured we'd be fine with those.

"Where to?" I asked.

"Women's clothing," Kayla said.

I followed her as we walked to the women's clothing section. Although it looked a mess and plenty picked over, Kayla sauntered and up and down the aisles finding items she thought she might salvage and tossing them into the cart. She stopped in front of one of the changing rooms and kicked off her sneakers.

"Can you see if you can find me a pair of shoes? Sneakers, or maybe hiking boots? I don't care as long as they don't smell like the river."

"Sure. What size?" I asked.

"Eight or nine," she said as she reached into the cart, selected a few items, and disappeared behind the door.

I did as she requested and found the shoe section. That, too, looters had picked over pretty good, but I scored a pair of lime green tennis shoes, and a pair of hikers from the men's department I thought might fit her. When I returned to the changing room, I saw the pile of clothes Kayla wore during her dunk in the river next to her shoes, and next to those were a few cotton shirts that she used to dry off. I waited patiently, and a few minutes later, the door opened, and she stepped out.

"Well? How do I look?" she asked.

"Much better," I said. And she did. Her clothes looked clean and fresh, from the bright white socks on her feet to the jeans to the navy blue T-shirt. "Except for the…"

Instead of trying to explain, I reached forward and removed a twig from her hair. I handed it to her. She shrugged and threw it on top of the discarded clothes.

"I get it. I need a proper bath. With shampoo, conditioner, and a nice soap. Sounds lovely, doesn't it?"

"I found these for you," I said as I held up the footwear options.

She considered the choice for a micro-second, then grabbed the men's hiking boots. She slipped back into the changing room and left the door open as she ripped the tags from the boots and put them on.

"I figure we should see if there's any food or water, then I want to check out the sporting goods section," she said when she got ready to go and stepped back in front of the cart.

Kayla walked through the store without a care in the world, like in the old days. I, on the other hand, stayed alert and peered down every row, expecting to encounter rovers at any moment. We snaked our way through the grocery aisles, but all we found was a small can of black olives.

Kayla opened the can the moment she found them. "Want one?" she asked, holding the can in my direction.

"No, thanks." I was hungry, but not hungry enough that I'd willingly eat a black olive.

As Kayla ate the olives, I pushed the cart to the sporting goods section. There, in the camping section, Kayla found a sleeping bag. Before I could question why she wanted it, she removed the bag from the nylon sack that held it and shoved the clothing from the cart into the sack, leaving the sleeping bag on the floor. Those before us had cleared out the rest of the camping section, along with the fishing and hunting sections. We could, however, have all the tennis rackets and home gym equipment we wanted.

"Find what you're looking for?" I asked.

"Come on," Kayla said.

I followed her along the back wall of the store and there she stopped in front of the bicycle section.

"Ta dah," she said, holding her hands out in front of her like she'd just made a rabbit appear from a hat.

"This is your idea? Bikes?" I asked.

"Yep."

"It's a good idea. Doesn't seem to be a lot of options here, though."

We looked over the rack and before us sat ten bikes, nine of which were meant for toddlers. That left one ten-speed, and that had two flat tires.

"I'll bet there's more in the back," Kayla said. "Why don't you go check, and I'll see if I can put air in these tires."

I put my backpack in the cart, fished out my flashlight, and went looking for the door that led to the stockroom. The skylights didn't extend to the back, so I switched on my light and wandered around the area. Like the front of the store, it was ransacked, but to my relief, I found a dozen unopened boxes of bicycles. I selected a man's mountain bike from the group and dragged it through the storeroom and out to where Kayla was putting air into a tire using a hand pump.

"How's it going?" I asked.

"The back one pumped up fine, but I think this one has a hole in the tube. I'll have to change it out."

"You have the equipment for that?"

Kayla pointed to the shelves behind her. The bicycle accessories section looked pretty much untouched.

"I think so. Will you need help with that?" she asked.

"Good question," I said. "Why don't you fix your flat, then jump in if I need you?"

"Fair enough."

While I ripped open the cardboard box, Kayla wandered over to the shelves and grabbed a new inner tube and several other items.

"Here, you'll probably need this."

I looked up, then accepted a small tool set Kayla handed me. It was the deluxe model and included a crescent wrench, two screwdrivers, pliers, and a socket set with six sockets.

"Thanks."

I removed all the bike parts from the box, lined them up neatly on the cardboard, and ripped open the plastic bag containing the assembly instructions.

"Can we go through the health and beauty department before we leave?" Kayla asked.

"Sure," I said without looking up from the manual. "What do you need?"

"While you were gone, I thought about the shampoo and soap. You know what I miss? Long hot showers. I'd love a hot shower. Or better yet, a spa day. A full day of pampering with a massage and a manicure and pedicure. Doesn't that sound fantastic?"

"Sure."

"What do you miss?"

I looked at the diagram of how to place the crank into the frame, but it seemed backward to me.

"Baker?"

I looked up at Kayla, and by the look on her face, she wasn't happy with me.

"I'm not ignoring you. Honest," I said. "Um, what do I miss? Ice cream."

Kayla laughed. "You have the entirety of human civilization to choose from, and you pick ice cream."

"Well, there are other things, I'm sure."

"Okay, like what?"

I thought for a moment. "Lots of stuff. Air conditioning. Drive-through restaurants. Cable television. Broadway plays. Baseball games. See. Lots of stuff. What do you miss?"

Kayla finished putting the tire on the rim and attached the pump to the valve.

"Oh, I don't know. Going to coffee shops. Art museums. Houseplants. Noise."

"Noise? What do you mean by that?" I asked.

"You know. Noise. When I was married, or visiting my parents, there was always a radio or a television on. Cars were always passing by the house, planes flying overhead. Motorcycles. The neighbor kid out playing in the yard. All that's gone, all that white noise we had all gotten used to. Now there's just quiet."

"Yeah, I know what you mean. Unless I'm with Pops or his dogs, there's practically no noise unless I'm down by my stream, or there are birds in the area. Aw, shit."

"What?"

"I just remembered. I had a really nice CD player in my truck. And my favorite road atlas. Now they're both up in flames."

Kayla reached over and patted my knee. "I'm sure we can find something around here. An atlas, at least. I'm not so sure about the CD player, but we'll see what we can do."

"Excellent."

Kayla finished pumping up her tire, declared the bike ready to go, and helped me finish my project. After my bike was together, we attached racks to the back of each of our bikes, then she secured the bag of new clothes to hers, and to mine I attached a small satchel in which I dumped the air pump, the toolset, and a few random bike repair parts.

From there, we walked our bikes to the book section, and although I couldn't find an atlas to replace the one I'd lost, I found road maps for each of the states we'd travel through. Not the best, but it was something.

In the health and beauty aisle, Kayla scavenged bottles of shampoo and body wash, along with toothpaste and toothbrushes, for both of us. I picked out a travel-sized can of shaving cream and a couple of razors for myself. Although it seemed most men ignored their facial hair in the new world, I preferred the look and feel of being as clean-shaven as possible. Once we squirreled away our items, we walked out into the sunshine, got on our bikes, and pedaled toward the interstate.

CHAPTER SIXTEEN

We put Vicksburg behind us and since the sun started to drop over our shoulders; we left the highway and found an abandoned barn to bunk down in. It looked like no one had used it in a few years, and it had a hole in the roof we needed to avoid in case it rained, but it seemed comfortable enough for one night.

"We should have kept that sleeping bag," I said as I got stabbed between the shoulder blades by a few tough pieces of straw.

"You don't like the thrill of camping? How did you sleep on the way here? In all the best hotels?" Kayla teased.

I chuckled. "No. I slept in the back of my mail truck. It was great. I had plenty of room to stretch out in there, and I didn't have to worry about things like bugs and the weather. Also, if I needed to, I could make a quick getaway."

Kayla laid down next to me, put her head on my shoulder, and draped her arm over my chest. "Do you want some of this blanket?" Kayla found the blanket draped over a stall door. The old blanket felt stiff, and it gave off an odor that not even a horse would tolerate.

"Nah, I'm good for now. Perhaps later if it gets colder. Or you might move over another couple of inches, and we could share body heat."

Without hesitation, Kayla shifted over a little and draped her leg over mine. I suspected I'd lose all sensation in that leg within ten minutes, but at the moment, I didn't care.

"Baker?"

"Yeah?"

"I'm glad you came for me." Kayla gave me a brief hug, and I sensed the electricity run through my body.

"Me too."

I don't know how long I stayed awake, but it was long enough to watch as the sky darkened, and the stars come out through the hole in the roof. As the night descended, Kayla's breathing deepened as she passed off to sleep, and she began to snore a sound that seemed more like a pleasant cat purr than an irritant. The night bugs came out, and based on the sounds of wings, I suspected we shared the barn with either an owl or bats.

Eventually, Kayla rolled over, and I took a moment to stretch my arms and legs before I rolled over too. I couldn't sleep if I was on my back, so I moved closer to Kayla and put my arm over her, becoming the big spoon. Soon, I exhaled, beat from a long day, and willed sleep to come.

I heard birds. When I opened my eyes and looked through the roof, the night sky had changed to a perfect light blue sky with not a cloud in sight. The second thing I noticed was that Kayla had gone. I sat up, experiencing the agony of the stiff muscles in my lower back. I felt three hundred years old as I struggled to my feet and tried to stretch away the kinks from my torso, arms and legs. Once I moved more like a human, I worked my way through the barn and stepped out into the morning sunshine. Two yards outside the barn, I found Kayla tending a small fire.

"Good morning," she said when she spotted me. "Breakfast will be ready soon."

"Great," I said. "What are we having?"

"Ham and cheese omelets, a side of bacon, biscuits, gravy, and fresh squeezed orange juice."

I grinned. "Sounds great. What are we really having?"

"One egg split between us, a tomato, and a handful of wild blackberries."

"Sounds even better. Anything I can do?"

"Yes. Come on over and sit down. Has that water cooled down?"

Off to the side sat a small camping pot filled with water. I felt the side, and although it wasn't hot, it was still warm.

"It's not too bad. Are we having tea?"

"No. We're having water. You ready to eat?"

"I am."

"I've only got one spoon. Do you have one?" Kayla asked.

"No. You eat first, then I'll use yours."

Kayla nodded and dug into the meal. I watched as she removed the small skillet from the fire and cut the egg in half. She ate her half and passed the skillet and spoon to me. The egg was unseasoned, but still delicious, and it only took me a few seconds to wolf it down. I placed the spoon in the skillet, and the skillet in the grass next to me.

"This is excellent," Kayla said as she bit into the tomato like an apple, the juice dribbling from her chin. "Want some?"

I waved her off. "No, you go ahead. I'm not much of a tomato person. They bother my stomach."

"Your loss," she said. "Eat these."

Kayla passed me a bandanna and when I opened it up, I saw the blackberries there, looking plump and juicy. I popped one into my mouth and bit down. The berry exploded into a flavorful delight. I slowed my chewing so I could savor it more, then swallowed it down.

"It is me, or does food taste better since the end of the world?" I asked.

Kayla finished the last of the tomato before she answered. "Now that you mention it, I think I noticed the same thing. I wonder why that is."

"Maybe it is because we fend for ourselves?" I questioned. "We appreciate the meal more?"

Kayla nodded. "Or maybe it's because it's all fresh now. Processed food is a thing of the past, unless you happen to find a can of something that someone else didn't. No more over-salted canned goods. No more high fructose corn syrup."

"What do you have against corn syrup? Even the name sounds delicious."

Kayla laughed and snorted. "You're such a goofball. Help me break camp, and let's get out of here."

I did as she asked. I poured the water from the pot into our water bottles and put out the fire while she headed to the stream behind the barn to wash the skillet. Afterward, we donned our backpacks, climbed on our bikes, and headed back toward the interstate.

"Baker?" Kayla asked as she rode by my side at a comfortable speed.

"Yeah?"

"How long do you think it will take us to bike back to your farm?"

I thought about it for a minute, but couldn't come up with a definitive answer without my favorite atlas. "I don't know. Ten days? Two weeks? We could probably do it, but I'd much rather find a ride."

"I'm glad you said that. Seriously, Baker, I think my butt would die if I needed to ride this thing halfway across the country."

I grinned. "It would only be about a quarter way across the country."

Kayla rolled her eyes at me and threw me a raspberry.

"What time do you think it is?" I asked.

"I don't know. Nine? Ten? Do you have an appointment you need to get to?"

"Not really. I was thinking more like a drive by."

"Fine by me. I've got nothing else going on today. Lead on, Baker."

We rode for an hour, and finally I guided her to an off-ramp and we rode through a small town. I stopped at the town's water tower and looked up. To my relief, it looked like any other normal water tower, and not one that inspired nightmares. I turned down one side street, followed by another, and finally pulled into a driveway. We rode most of the way and when the house was within sight, we both dismounted and walked our bikes. I leaned mine against an apple tree and let my backpack fall from my shoulders. Before I could step toward the house, the screen door screeched open, and Jasmine erupted from it.

"Baker! What are you doing here?"

She ran at me, then fell into the hug that I offered.

"I'm headed home and thought I'd drop by and say hello. This is my friend I was telling you about. Jasmine, this is Kayla. Kayla, Jasmine."

Jasmine released me and gave Kayla a hug. "You didn't tell me she was so pretty."

I watched Kayla's cheeks redden with embarrassment.

"Is your dad home?" I asked.

Jasmine shook her head. "Naw, he's out hunting with Mr. Cooper. Mama's home, though. You should come in. She'll be happy to see you."

I let Jasmine escort us into the house, and I introduced Kayla to Etta, Jasmine's mother.

"Sugar, I'm so pleased to meet you," Etta said, taking Kayla into a hug exactly as Jasmine had done. At first, Kayla took a tentative step back, but then relented to the inevitable. "Reggie's out hunting. He should be back in an hour or so, then you can have a good meal with us. Assuming that he can bag something bigger than a squirrel." Etta started to laugh so hard she nearly folded herself in two, doubling over. Jasmine laughed as well, so I suspected it was a family joke Kayla and I weren't privy to.

"I don't know," I said. "We've got a lot of miles to go."

Jasmine's laughter stopped, and she quickly angered with me. "Baker! You can't go anywhere. Your bike tires are flat."

I shook my head. "No, they aren't."

Jasmine took a small pocketknife from her rear pocket and waved it in the air. "Well, they will be."

"Jasmine!" Etta yelled. "Put that away, child. Baker was just teasing you. Tell her."

I smiled and nodded. "Of course, we'll stick around for a bit. I'm hoping Reggie can find us something to drive."

"He might," Etta said. "But before we worry about that, I have to ask. Kayla, why do you have so much mud in your hair?"

There was a mirror to Kayla's left, and she turned to take in her reflection.

"Baker. Why didn't you tell me I looked this bad?"

I shrugged. "I think you look fine."

"Well, she don't, Baker. Time for flattery is over, and honesty is what's needed. And I know we just met, but, Sugar, you smell like a wet dog. Jasmine, take this woman over to the public showers and make sure she gets two. Tell them to put it on our tab."

"You don't have to pay for me," Kayla protested.

Etta put her hand up, blocking Kayla's next sentence. "Hush now. Baker's already earned enough for this family to cover a million showers. You go on and follow Jasmine."

Jasmine left the room and returned a few moments later with a fresh towel and a basket of shower sundries. "Do you need fresh clothes?"

Kayla shook her said. "No. I have some on my bike. Let's go."

I stood with Etta in the living room and watched through the door as Kayla gathered what she needed and walked with Jasmine down the driveway.

"Does she know what happened here?" Etta asked without looking at me.

"No."

"Are you going to tell her?"

I hesitated. "To be honest, I'd rather forget about everything I saw and did here and never speak or even think about it again. But, if it comes up somehow, I'd prefer she knows the truth."

Etta nodded. "You're a good man, Baker. Now come on in the kitchen and keep me company while I tend to the vegetables."

I followed her into the kitchen and took a seat at the table. When she said she needed to tend to the vegetables, I pictured her needing to shuck some corn, but instead I walked into a full-fledged canning operation. Against one wall were crates of vegetables stacked five feet high. The top one looked filled to the brim with green beans, the next one down had a shoot of asparagus sticking out between the slats, and the third contained okra. What the bottom one held; I couldn't tell. Every other space was taken up by canning jars, including every inch of the kitchen table and the counters.

"What's going on here?" I asked.

"I'm on the canning committee," Etta said. "Everyone in town has a job they do to contribute to the community. We're responsible for making sure we have food through the winter. Think you can help out?"

"Sure. What do you want me to do?"

Etta looked around for an empty crate and in it stored several jars from the table, creating me a workspace. Then, in front of me, she placed a massive bowl. Next to my chair, she dropped a burlap sack, then to my other side placed a kitchen-sized plastic garbage pail lined with another burlap sack.

"Shell the peas. The peas go in the bowl, pods go in the sack."

I opened the sack next to me and took out a pea. "Sugar snap? I grow these. Can't you can them whole?"

"Don't turn out as good. Besides, we use the pods for the livestock. Pea pods are great for horses and cows. And pigs, but they'll eat just about anything." Etta turned her attention back to the stove where she was boiling empty jars in large pots of water.

I cracked the pod open, pushed the peas out with my thumb, and dropped the pod in the bin.

"Where did you get all of these veggies?" I asked as I reached for the next pod.

"Several people around town have gardens, and there are a couple of farmers nearby who provide them. We set aside about half for people to eat fresh, and can the other half for later."

"Where do you store them?"

"Down on Main Street, there's the grocery store. Used to be a little thing that just carried the minimum of essentials, but the men knocked through the wall to the connected building to expand the space. In the smaller space, we keep all the fresh food, and in the other, we keep the canned goods."

"How do you pay?"

Etta laughed. "You don't. Not for food, anyway. No one goes hungry here. The store doesn't even have a lock on the door. Well, it has a latch on the outside to keep the door from blowing open, but it's never locked. In this town, if you want some food, you just go there and get what you need. That's the key, though, just taking what you need."

"Why's that?"

"Well, in the beginning, we had a problem with people hoarding food. Some folks were getting fat, while others couldn't rub two carrots together. That wasn't right, so we changed it to the way we have now. As long as people don't get greedy, it'll work just fine."

"But you have to pay for a shower?" I asked as I nimbly worked another few peas free from a pod.

"Showers are a luxury. Some folks still have running water, like myself, but others don't, so there's a place down near the tower where they built a public shower. It's gravity fed, and they heat the water by fire. It takes extra effort, so it's a charge. Just like other goods, like batteries, books, some clothing, tools. We have a group on the scavenger committee who go out to look for things during the day, and those items have a price for them."

"How do you pay? With cash?"

"No. With points. For everything you contribute, you earn points. Like I get ten points a jar for everything I can, or the growers get a point for every pound of vegetables they produce. All your points go into the book, and then when you need something, like a new bar of soap, let's say, the points the bar of soap is worth get deducted from your tally."

"How do you know how much soap is worth?" I asked.

"There's a committee for that, too. Whatever is produced or brought in goes to the committee first, and they either enter it into inventory, or assign points to it if it's a new item. When I take these jars over to the store, someone there will count what I have and give me credit for them."

"Sounds like an excellent system for a small town."

Etta nodded. "It works for us." She turned around to check on my progress, put her hands on her hips, and shook her head at me. "You need to step up your speed, or we'll be canning those peas until Gabriel blows his horn."

I laughed and Etta pulled up a chair of her own and dipped her hand into the sack and retrieved a half dozen pods. She worked her way through five of them before I finished one. She moved in for a second handful and got to work while I attempted, without success, to follow her cadence. Etta went through the motions of opening and emptying the pods the same way every time, with no wasted movement or effort like she was a pea removal robot.

She smiled at my vain attempt to keep pace with her. "It's all practice. Once you've shelled a million pods, you'll have it down, too."

We both looked up as we both heard the front screen door open, then slam shut.

"Honey, there are bikes out in the yard. You know anything about that?" Reggie boomed. A minute later, he appeared in the kitchen, looking happier and more at peace than the last time I'd seen him.

"Baker!" he said as he approached. Before I had the chance to stand, he came over and wrapped me in a bear hug. Hugging, I determined, was a well-ingrained Sherman family trait. "What brings you here?"

"I'm headed home to Virginia," I said, still working through the pile of peas before me.

"So, you found your friend?"

"Jasmine took her for a shower. She was a little… ripe," Etta said.

She got up to attend to the boiling jars and Reggie slid into the seat she vacated and retrieved some peas for himself. He checked to make sure she wasn't looking, then popped one into his mouth. It crunched between his teeth, and he smiled as he ate it.

"I heard that," Etta said without turning back around.

"How was the hunt?" I asked.

"There's half a deer hanging out there, so we'll be dining on venison steaks tonight. You are staying for dinner, aren't you?" Reggie worked his way through the peas at almost the same speed as Etta, without even looking at what he was doing as he went.

"Of course they are, dear," Etta answered before I had a chance to decline.

I smiled and nodded.

The screen door screeched again.

"That must be Willie," Reggie said. "He'll be happy to see you."

"Willie's staying with a friend tonight, so that's not him."

A few seconds later, Jasmine entered the crowded kitchen with Kayla right on her heels. After Jasmine introduced Kayla to her father, Kayla moved to me and hugged me from behind. The Sherman family trait seemed to be contagious.

CHAPTER SEVENTEEN

We ate dinner outdoors around a fire pit, and we ate like royalty. Reggie had grilled the venison steaks while Etta raided the fresh vegetables in the kitchen and prepared from that sauteed green beans, fried okra, which I admit I didn't care for since I'd never been an okra fan, and fresh corn on the cob. To go with that, we had fresh-baked corn bread, and the freshest lemonade I'd ever tasted.

Conversation was light during the meal itself and limited to mostly words of praise for the delicious food, but eventually the feast ended, and Kayla and I collected the plates, took them to the kitchen, and returned to our seats.

"Thank you so much for the meal," Kayla said.

"Oh, Sugar, it's our pleasure," Etta said. "It's not often we get such good company during supper."

I downed the last of my lemonade and set the plastic cup on the ground next to my chair leg. "Reggie, I hate to ask, but do you think there's any transportation around here I could have? Car? Bus? Van? Anything? It doesn't have to be pretty; it only has to roll."

Reggie grinned at me. "Don't want to ride a ten-speed through five more states?"

"I would, but you know…" I cocked my head in Kayla's direction and raised an eyebrow.

"Baker, don't be a jerk," Kayla said as she playfully punched me in the shoulder.

"So that tells me she's the smart one of the pair," Reggie said. He pondered it for a moment. "I guess I might be able to help you out. I'll check it out in the morning. Is that okay?"

I nodded. "Can I ask for one additional favor? Could you let us bunk down in your shed for the night?"

"Oh, no, no," Etta said. "No way. You'll be in the house with us."

"I just didn't want to put you out."

"Nonsense. You can sleep in Willie's room. He's not using it tonight. The bed's only a twin, so if that won't work for the two of you, one of you can settle in on the couch."

"That's perfect, thank you," Kayla said.

Off in the distance, the frogs started to sing their nighttime chorus, and a hush fell over our group.

"So, Baker," Etta said, breaking the silence. "How did you two meet?"

I glanced at Kayla, who stared me down, interested in whether I actually remembered the truth or if I would spin a tale that varied widely from what actually happened.

I looked from Etta to Reggie to Jasmine and back at Kayla, who gave me one of her patented sweet smiles.

"Well? We're waiting," she said, almost in a whisper.

I sat back in my chair and rubbed my hands on my pants. "Well, where do I begin?"

"How about at the beginning?" Reggie offered.

"Maybe he doesn't remember," Kayla said. "It was a long, long time ago."

I glanced at her and threw her a weak smile, sensing that she was trying to dig me out of the hole.

"Come on, Baker. I'm sure you remember something about it. Just give us the overview," Etta pressed.

"Well," I started, "it was a long, long time ago, like Kayla said, and I don't remember everything about it, but here's what I do remember."

I paused for an extended moment. Everyone probably assumed it was to search my memory banks, but it was only a bit of well-placed drama on my part.

"It was a Sunday night, I remember. We were both at a professional conference, at one of those mixer things that we were obligated to go to. For me, anyway, it was one of those events where I planned on staying only long enough to be seen by the right people and then pretend I needed to use the bathroom and disappear for the rest of the night. Then, Kayla and the group of people she was with got introduced to the group of people I was with, and we all did that thing where we step in and shake hands, you know?"

I paused for a moment. More drama on my part.

"And?" Jasmine said, ready for the story to move along.

"And then we shook hands, and I noticed five things."

"Five?" Etta said. "Not just one, but five?"

I nodded and counted them off on my fingers. "The first was her eyes. I'd learned somewhere that you should always look someone in the eyes, and when I looked into hers, I was like, wow. They were bright green or sometimes hazel, based on the light, but regardless of the color, the sparkle, the life behind them was intense and captivating."

I glanced over at Kayla, and she shot me an uncomfortable smile.

"The second thing was the handshake itself. Her hand felt soft in mine, yet the shake itself was firm and strong. The third was I looked down a second and noticed the scar."

"What scar?" Reggie interrupted.

"She's got a scar on her right hand. In the web between her thumb and forefinger. About an inch long."

Reggie glanced over at Kayla. She blushed and held her hand up for all to see.

Etta got up from her chair, took Kayla's hand in hers, and scrutinized it. "You mean this little thing? How'd you even see it?"

I shrugged as Etta took her seat. "Don't know. I just did. I saw that scar, and I wanted to know the background, the story of how it came to be, how that one flaw came to be on such a perfect hand."

"Oh please," Kayla said.

"Hey, you wanted me to tell the story, right?"

"Okay. What was the fourth?" Jasmine asked.

"The electricity," I said, turning my attention to the teen, who was literally sitting on the edge of her seat. "The second we made contact, I received this bolt of energy that rushed from my hand right up to my shoulder and right down to my toes. It was like lightning had struck me."

"That was static," Kayla protested, although everyone ignored her comment.

"And the fifth thing?" Etta said.

"The fifth thing," I said, dropping my voice to just above a whisper and leaning forward in my seat as if sharing the biggest of secrets. On instinct, the four others leaned forward, too. "The fifth thing was, I never wanted to let her hand go."

The reactions to my statement varied. Reggie laughed, sat back, and crossed his legs. Etta smiled widely and patted my knee. Jasmine put her hand over her heart like it was the sweetest thing she'd ever heard. Kayla rolled her eyes at me, which was a very Kayla thing to do.

"We got drinks. She had a red wine, I got a Diet Coke, and we found a quiet corner and chatted for a while about all the things that people do when they first meet. Backgrounds, families, jobs, all that kind of surface stuff. We did that for, what, a half hour?"

Kayla sighed.

"Okay. It was more like three hours. At one point we looked up and most of the bar was empty, except for the poor staff waiting for us to clear out so they could clean up. So, then we left the bar."

"Did you go back to your room and have sex?" Jasmine blurted. She looked at Reggie and Etta as soon as the words escaped her, then covered her mouth with both hands. "Sorry."

I laughed. "No. We didn't. By that time, it was almost midnight, and we both needed to be up early for seminars. We walked to the elevator together and got in. She got off at the fourth floor, and I never left the car when we said goodnight. I headed to bed all alone. When I woke up the next morning, I was already running late, so I got dressed and rushed down to the meeting room. I got there just as the session began and noticed Kayla sitting in the back row, right by the door with an empty seat right next to her. So, I asked if I could sit down, and she said she'd been saving the seat for me."

"How sweet," Etta said. "What happened next?"

"Boredom," Kayla said. "Pure and complete boredom for like four straight hours."

"It was the seminar, not me," I explained. "Then we got released for lunch, and I asked her to join me, and she took me up on that offer. Down the street from the convention center we found this little hole in the wall Chinese place. We ate for an hour, again, sharing small talk, and when the break was over, Kayla suggested we skip the afternoon sessions and go to the park instead."

"So, what did you do?" Jasmine asked.

"I went with her to the park. How is doing otherwise even an option? There, we found a bench under a tall oak tree and talked more. At one point, we spotted an ice cream vendor up the block, so we headed there for a treat. Turns out we both liked the same ice cream. Mint chocolate chip. Go figure. Dessert in hand, we walked around the park for a while before settling in on a bench for more conversation."

"This is a boring story," Jasmine interjected.

"Jazz," Etta scolded.

"Well, it is," Jasmine said, folding her arms to her chest.

"What would make it more exciting for you?" I asked.

Jasmine dropped her defense posture and put her hands on her knees. "Did you kiss her?"

"Jazz!" Etta repeated.

Jasmine paid no attention to her mother and instead stared at me.

"No, actually, I never have," I admitted.

"Do you want to?" Jasmine asked.

I smiled, but didn't answer.

"You do! Baker!"

"Jasmine, that's enough," Etta said. "Mr. Baker, I apologize for my child's behavior."

"It's really not a problem," I said. "We've never kissed, but yes, I want to. Actually, I've dreamed of it often over the last fifteen years or so." Everyone stared at me when I finished my confession. I didn't look over at Kayla, so I didn't know what her reaction was. Since I was already deep in the hole I dug for myself, I kept going.

"To tell you the truth, I've loved her since the moment I first looked into her eyes. That love runs deep, and often feels more like magic than reality to me. Until we met, I never really believed in the concept of a soul mate. But now? I guarantee you they exist, and that Kayla is mine."

When I finished, no one spoke. Even the frogs fell silent. The moment hung in the air like a dense fog. After almost a minute, I leaned forward and whispered to Jasmine. "Is she looking at me?"

Jasmine nodded.

"Does she look irritated?"

Jasmine smiled and shook her head no. I nodded and sat back in my chair. A moment later, I felt Kayla's hand reaching for mine, and within a moment, our fingers intertwined, and she gave me a light squeeze.

"But, I don't understand," Etta said. "If y'all are meant to be together, why aren't you together?"

I thought about it for a moment, then gave an extended sigh.

"That's an excellent question. One I'm not sure I have a suitable answer to. When we met, I was in the middle of an unhappy relationship, and she was in a happy marriage, so the timing was bad for both of us. And, until just now, I'd never really acknowledged my true feelings."

"You've known her for fifteen years, and never told her you loved her?" Reggie asked.

I nodded.

"Can I ask a follow-up question?" Reggie asked.

"Of course," I said.

"Are you stupid, son?"

"Reginald!" Etta yelled, smacking her husband on her leg.

I started to laugh, as did Kayla and Jasmine, but a look of fury passed over Etta's face.

"I think perhaps I am," I admitted. "At least I was smart enough to keep her close over the years. Texts, phone calls, birthday cards. Granted, there were unspoken words between us, probably the most important words, but I don't think there were many times when we didn't talk every day, were there?"

I looked at Kayla for an answer. "That's true. Just about every day we talked until the world fell apart."

"What did you do in the before times?" Etta asked Kayla.

"Well, when I first met Baker, I worked in finance. I hate to brag, but I was on the fast track to becoming the first woman executive officer the company ever had. Then I got into something a little less lucrative, and I've been doing that the last few years."

"What did you get into?" Reggie asked.

Kayla mumbled an answer.

"What was that?" Reggie asked.

"I ran an animal rescue," Kayla said louder. Her cheeks reddened with embarrassment, and she pulled her feet off the ground and sat on them.

"How did you get into that line of work?" Etta asked. "That seems like quite the jump from finance."

"Well, I was working late one night, and the news came on. Halfway through they played this human-interest story about a woman who ran a shelter, but she had to give it up due to health reasons. Since there was no one else to step in, the county was going to shut it down. All throughout the segment they kept showing video of all those animals. That night when I went to bed I couldn't sleep. All I kept thinking about were all those sad looking creatures. The next day was a Saturday, so I went out to see that lady, and she showed me around the place, and I couldn't get enough. So, we worked out a deal. She would take care of the business side, and I would tend to the operational side, including caring for all those animals."

"What kind of animals do you have?" Jasmine asked.

"We had mostly cats and dogs. But we also cared for other things. We had a baby opossum come through, and a tortoise, and a half dozen of those fainting goats."

"Oh, how cute, I love those!" Jasmine squealed with delight.

"Me too," Kayla said.

"What did your husband say about all that?" Reggie asked. "He couldn't have been too happy with you going from the fast track to a farmer."

"Unhappy is an understatement. He got super p… angry with me. But, I stuck up for myself. And I would do it again if I had the chance."

"Why?" Etta asked.

"Because all I was making for the corporation was money. But with those animals, I could make a difference, one cat or dog or goat at a time."

"Bah," Reggie scoffed.

"Reggie!" Etta smacked him on the knee. "Did you forget the good book? Says right there in Proverbs that the righteous care for the needs of their animals. This lady here does God's work, and that makes her okay in my book."

Reggie looked taken aback, so he changed the subject. "So, how did you stay in contact?" Reggie asked.

"When I noticed the country was going to slide off the edge of the cliff, I sent her a satellite phone. It's funny. I didn't mind losing my job, or my comfortable life, or all the struggles I've had to go through from the beginning of the end until now. But the thought of being out of contact with Kayla forever? That's what kept me awake at night."

Kayla gave my fingers another squeeze, and I gave her a light squeeze in return.

"What about the promise?" Jasmine asked. "When you were here last, you kept talking about a promise. What was that about?"

"Well, when it was time for us to part, when we left the conference, headed back to our respective homes, I promised her that if she needed me for anything, I'd be there for her. Regardless of what it was, or where we were at the time."

Reggie nodded. "So, when she called you after she got left alone, you put your life on pause in Virginia to go and get her."

I nodded. "That's a simple way to put it."

"Considering the circumstances, I'm not sure there are many who would have kept that particular promise," he said.

"But he did," Kayla said. "He probably saved my life in the process."

Reggie didn't say anything, but instead shot a glance at Etta, who shook her head so slightly I barely caught it. I hoped Kayla hadn't caught it at all.

Once again, silence smothered the conversation, and the words drifted away on a light breeze that blew through.

"Well, speaking of promises, I think I have a vehicle for you," Reggie said. "It's not a limousine, but I think it will get you home. We'll head out first thing in the morning and pick it up."

"Great, thanks," I said.

"Yes, thank you. We appreciate it," Kayla added.

"It's getting late. I should be getting to bed," Etta said. "Morning comes early around here, and I got a lot of canning to do tomorrow."

"Will you be needing my help with that?" I asked.

Etta stood, walked over to me, and gave me a kiss on the forehead. "Bless you for offering Baker, but to be honest, you're slowing me down." With a laugh, Etta headed into the house with Reggie on her heels.

"You coming in?" Jasmine asked as she rose.

"Right behind you," I said.

Jasmine gave Kayla and me each a hug and headed for the house.

"You sure made some good friends here, Baker," Kayla said, letting go of my hand. "How did you manage to make such an impact on these people just by passing through town on the way to get me?"

"Well," I started, then paused. I knew I should tell her, but didn't know where to start, nor how much detail to dive into.

"Oh, wait. Want to hear something interesting that happened to me today?" she asked.

"Of course. Tell me."

"Well, Jasmine and I walked to town, which isn't far from here. There's a spot there where the fire department and police department share the same block by the water tower. Anyway, they have the public shower setup behind the fire department. They've got quite the setup over there. They heat the water, and pump it to an overhead reservoir, and it is gravity fed from there. There was someone in line in front of me, so as I waited my turn, the person operating the shower started making small talk with Jasmine, and that turned into a discussion about who I was and who I was with. And you won't believe this, but the person running the shower had nothing but high praise for you, too. As did the person in the shower ahead of me. As did the person who stopped to say hello to Jasmine. So, tell me, Baker. How is it everyone in this little town knows you?"

I looked Kayla in the eyes and opened my mouth to speak. Before I could utter a word, she put her index finger against my lips to silence me.

"The things you didn't want to talk about all happened here, didn't they?"

I nodded, her finger still on my lips.

"And you'd really prefer to keep it all to yourself for now?"

I nodded again.

"Okay. To tell you the truth, on one hand, I'm irritated with you for taking such a colossal risk. Who knows what would have happened to you had things not turned out the way they did? But, on the other hand, I'm really proud of you. You put your life on the line. And it's one thing to do it for me all because of a silly promise, but quite another to do it for a bunch of strangers."

"I wanted to tell you," I said. "I wanted to tell you everything."

"Despite what I heard from Jasmine and her friends, I think I didn't get the complete story from them. In fact, I suspect that something horrible went on here that everyone wants to forget. Including you."

I hesitated, then nodded.

"So, here's the deal. We're going to drop it right here on this lawn. I'm not going to bring it up again, nor am I going to pressure you to. If you want to tell me everything, I'll listen, but you have to want to. Is that a fair deal?"

I exhaled. I didn't realize I'd been holding my breath. "Yes. It is."

"Okay." Kayla stood, grabbed my hand, and pulled me to my feet. "Come on, hero. Let's go get some sleep."

CHAPTER EIGHTEEN

The next morning when Reggie and I pulled into the driveway on a machine that made enough noise to be picked up the next state over, Etta, Kayla, and Jasmine rushed from the house and joined us in the yard. I noticed Willie had made it home, and when I got off the machine, he came over and greeted me with a handshake and a bro-hug.

"What on earth is that?" Kayla asked.

"It's a motorcycle. Reggie found it for us," I said.

Reggie had some difficulty climbing out of the sidecar, and I thought the entire machine would tip over when he did, but it bounced back on its mostly bald tires.

"It was in that old red barn over near the Jackson's place."

"You should have left it there," Etta said.

I shook my head. "Nah, this will work great. It's got room for both of us and our gear, and it should get us to Virginia fine."

"As long as you treat it nice," Reggie said.

I nodded.

"And check that oil every hundred miles or so."

"I know."

Reggie was about to add something else, but I stopped him. Even though I was over-confident that the old machine would get us to Virginia. I figured if it even got us as far as the Alabama state line I'd be good with that. Every little bit of not having to walk or pedal helped.

After an hour of repacking and reorganizing so everything would either fit on the motorcycle or in the sidecar, we were ready to hit the road.

"I hope we meet again someday, Baker," Etta said as she drew me into an embrace.

"I hope so, too," I said in her ear. She gave me a peck on the cheek, let me go, and moved onto Kayla while Reggie stepped in to take her place. He took my hand in his and brought me in for a hug.

"You're always welcome here," Reggie said.

"And if you're ever up in Virginia, there's a place there for you," I said, meaning every word.

Reggie sighed, and when he exhaled, I noticed his body shrank. "I suspect this is probably goodbye forever," he whispered.

I didn't speak, and after an awkward ten-second silence I wanted to respond to say otherwise, but in my heart, I realized it was the case.

"Take care of yourself. And your lady," Reggie said. He gave me a last squeeze, let me loose, said farewell to Kayla, and followed Etta into the house.

Willie stood off near the door, hands in pockets, and I thought he'd follow his parents into the house. He surprised me though, when he ran toward me at full speed and jumped into my arms and wrapped his arms around my neck, almost making me fall over in the process. Willie started to say something but choked on his words. He let go, dropped to the ground, and sprinted toward the house.

Etta came out a second later and returned to Kayla. "I'm sorry we didn't get a chance to know each other better, but I have a feeling that you're a really good person, especially deep down where it counts. I want you to have this."

Etta handed something to Kayla, who held the item in her hand. I looked over and saw it was a pin. A silver dove.

"I can't take this," Kayla protested.

"You will. And may the Lord watch over you and Baker."

Etta gave Kayla another kiss and hug and returned to the house.

"You really have to go, Baker?" I turned around and spotted Jasmine standing next to the motorcycle. She did not try to hide or wipe away her flowing tears.

"Yeah, kiddo, we do. We have our own home to go to, and I have an elderly neighbor who needs my help with things around the homestead."

She smiled just a bit. "Always gotta be playing the hero."

I shook my head. "Look, I'm no hero, Jasmine. I simply try to do the right thing when the situation calls for it."

Jasmine stepped over and I pulled her into a hug. "You'll always be my hero, Baker."

I kissed Jasmine on the head, and after a minute she pulled away, said goodbye to Kayla, and headed toward the house. She was halfway there when she stopped and turned around.

"Baker's still a silly name," Jasmine called out. Then she waved, and a second later, she disappeared into the house.

"No sillier than Jasmine," I whispered to myself.

"Come on, cowboy, let's saddle up," Kayla said, tugging me by the shirt as she headed to the motorcycle.

I nodded and let Kayla guide me to the bike. Once she settled into the sidecar and we had the gear stowed, I got on the bike and brought the beast to life. At first it coughed, but then kicked in. I put it into gear, and with a shudder, I turned it around and headed for the road.

I made my way through the small town, returning waves from the people we passed on the way to the interstate. Deep down, I was happy to leave, although I knew I'd miss the Sherman family. Before we even reached the highway, the motorcycle began to smoke, so I pulled into the gas station where

I first met Jasmine and checked the oil. Sure enough, the dipstick told me the bike was already low. I showed Kayla how to get gas from the underground tank, and while she did that, I went into the station itself and rummaged around until I found an entire case of oil. Since I didn't have the owner's manual and didn't know for certain which brand of bike it was, I didn't exactly know which type of oil it was supposed to take. Not that it mattered, since I only had one choice. The case contained twelve quarts, and the motorcycle sucked up two. When we found a home for the other ten quarts in the sidecar, we got back on the road.

Although Reggie recommended that we stop every hundred miles to check the oil, we paused every thirty minutes, and each time the machine ate another quart. When we got a few miles east of Tuscaloosa, I pulled the bike off the highway, parked it under an overpass, and dismounted.

"What are we stopping for?" Kayla asked.

"Couple of things. First, I need to pee. Could you check the oil while I take care of business?"

Kayla nodded then exited the sidecar while I ventured off behind a concrete bridge support to be more discreet. When I returned, Kayla was emptying another quart into the bike. She put the lid back on the bottle and set the bottle on a guardrail.

"I'm going to take my turn, too," Kayla said as she wandered off to take care of things.

While she was gone, I rummaged around in my backpack for the map of Alabama I had stored in there. Not wanting to repeat the encounter I had in Birmingham, I looked for an alternate route and decided to take the interstate bypass that would swing us southeast around the city.

"What are you doing?" Kayla asked when she caught me double-checking the route.

"Well, I had a little trouble when I came through Birmingham a few days ago," I said, hoping to leave it at that. Kayla stared at me until I told the story of my encounter, holding nothing back from her.

Once I gave her the alternate route, she nodded, then climbed back into the sidecar. An hour later, we arrived at the bypass, and I took it and then stopped the bike, got off, and added another quart of oil.

"How many of these do we have left?" I asked, holding up the empty bottle.

"Two," Kayla answered. "We'll need to find more."

I nodded. "Yeah. Let's get to the far side of Birmingham first."

I got back on the bike and fired it up. As usual, it sounded like a jet engine with a freight train horn attached.

"I wish we had a quieter bike!" I screamed through the noise.

"Then find us a Honda next time," Kayla screamed back.

I grinned, put it into gear, and continued the journey. After almost an hour, we cleared the city, and I spotted the sign for I-59, which was only a mile ahead when I noticed the engine started smoking again. I pulled over and shut off the engine.

"Damn," I said as Kayla handed me the last two quarts of oil. "This thing is becoming more trouble than it's worth."

"There's a gas station over there," Kayla said, pointing off to our right. "Next exit. We can find more oil, or hopefully a new vehicle."

"Good idea," I said. I topped off the oil, tossed the empty bottles, and fired up the machine.

I headed toward the exit ramp and was most of the way down it when I spotted the obstruction. Across the road was what appeared to be a home-made version of police stop sticks. Although I was going only fifty miles an hour and tried to stop as soon as I spotted them, I hit them almost at full speed. All three tires popped almost at once, and the bike shook violently. Without the sidecar, I know I would have flipped the bike at once, and I hoped the extra mass would keep us grounded until I could stop us. As I tried to stop, I noticed piles of bricks placed randomly on the road, and when I swerved to avoid one pile, the sidecar tire struck a random brick and I lost control of the bike. I sensed us go airborne, Kayla screamed, then darkness fell.

*

"Baker? Come on Baker. Wake up."

I opened my eyes and saw Kayla crouched down beside me.

"What happened?" I asked.

"We crashed. I think there are people coming. We need to get out of here."

I tried to move, but couldn't. "Kayla, I can't move. I think my back got busted."

"No. You're underneath the bike. Hold on."

Kayla stood and pushed at the machine. When she did, all my joints exploded in pain, but I was happy to experience it. At least I wasn't paralyzed as I originally thought.

"Can you help me?" Kayla asked.

I was lying face down and I tried to get my arms under me to push up, but I had zero leverage. I tried to roll over, but couldn't do that, either.

"Come on, Baker, they're getting closer."

"It's no use," I said. "Take my backpack. You still have the rifle?"

"It's in the road. I dropped it when we flipped,"

I worked to slip out of the backpack, then pushed it out at her. "Take this, grab the rifle, and go hide in the trees. I'll play dead until they leave."

"Baker, I can't leave—"

"GO!" I screamed.

Kayla hesitated for a moment, then picked up my pack. Although she stepped out of my sight line, I heard the rifle scrape on the concrete when she picked it up, and she came back into my view as she ran across the road, climbed over the guardrail, and headed into a small copse of trees next to the road. I tried again to push the bike off of me, but I couldn't. Next, I attempted to slide out from underneath it, but that didn't work either. I stopped struggling when I overheard voices.

"Look here," a man said. "We got one."

Although I closed my eyes and tried to play dead, my ruse stopped when I got slapped on the side of my head, and my eyes instinctively opened, and I twitched. Above me were three men who looked to be in their early twenties staring at me.

"He got anything good on him?" A fourth voice said.

"Can't tell. He's under the bike," the man closest to me said. He wore a dirty trucker's hat and from the green on his teeth and the wafted odor I got when he spoke, I doubted he owned a toothbrush.

"Well, jeez, Earl, why don't you idiots get him out of there and check what he has on him?"

The three men disappeared from my view and a moment later, the bike's weight left my body. I stretched my legs and wiggled my toes, happy to do both. A second later, Earl came back and started patting me down.

"Shit, he ain't got nothing on him," Earl said.

"Get him up."

Earl grabbed me under one armpit, another man grabbed me by the other, and hoisted me up with ease.

"Where you got the stuff?" the leader said, stepping into view. This one wore scuffed cowboy boots, dirty jeans, and denim jacket, even though the temperature hovered in the high eighties.

"What stuff?" I asked.

Rather than answer, the man hit me directly in the stomach with full force. The men holding me let go, and I fell to the ground, gasping for air. As I tried to catch my breath, the leader stepped forward, lined me up like a soccer ball, and kicked me in the head. I flew backwards and watched stars explode when the back of my head hit the concrete. I rolled onto my side, and the man kicked me twice more in the stomach. Rather than protect those areas, I put my arms by my head in a feeble attempt to protect my face. He kicked me a third time, and I wheezed, then threw up.

"He done puked on your boots!" Earl said.

"I know that, you idiot. Get him up again."

Earl and his friend grabbed me by the arms. This time, they had to support my full weight. My legs felt like overcooked noodles, and I couldn't support myself.

"Hey,"

I looked forward at the leader just in time to spot his fist headed my way. He wanted to hit me in the nose, but I dropped my head in time and took the shot right between the eyes instead. The force of the blow made me stumble a few steps backward, but the men held on and moved me forward again. I heard a click and lifted my head and saw the switchblade the leader waved in front of my face.

"Time to say goodbye," he said.

"Hey!" Kayla shouted from the trees.

"See, I told you there was another one," Earl said.

"Let him go!" Kayla shouted again.

"Okay. We will," the leader said.

I saw him thrust once with the knife, then he backed away from me.

"You heard her. Let him go and go get that woman," the leader said.

Earl and his friend released me, and to my surprise, I stayed on my feet. Something didn't feel right, so I touched my abdomen and looked at my hands. It was all wrong. Instead of two hands, there were four, and all of them seemed covered in blood. Kayla yelled something else I didn't make out. Then a gunshot pierced my ears, and the ricochet skipped on the concrete nearby. I attempted to turn, staggered twice, and dropped to the ground.

*

Something was squeaking. An annoying squeak. Not like a mouse, more like that one shopping cart wheel that never worked quite right and when it wasn't squeaking, froze up or turned sideways. I opened my eyes and saw fuzzy starlight above me. At first, I thought the stars were moving, then realized it was me. I tried to move, but couldn't. Instead, I groaned.

I stopped. So did the squeaking. A moment later, Kayla stood above me.

"Hey, there," she said.

"I thought you got shot," I mumbled.

"That was me doing the shooting. Hold tight, we're almost there."

She left, and a moment later, I started moving again. I watched the stars and waited. What seemed an eternity later, I saw we were under a building. Then Kayla opened the door and pulled me inside, closing and locking the door behind us. I looked around and discovered we were inside an abandoned Mexican restaurant that smelled like old shoes. Kayle bent over me, did something, and I suddenly seemed free.

"Can you stand?" she asked.

"Let's find out."

It was a struggle, but she helped me to my feet and got me into a chair. I looked at the floor and there I saw a mechanic's creeper and several bungee cords. Attached to the front of the creeper was a rope, and I put the pieces together. Kayla had gone to the gas station, found the creeper, tied me to it, and used it to transport me. Clever girl.

"How do you feel?" she asked.

"Bad. How do I look?"

"Worse."

"Is there anything to drink?"

"Don't know. I'll be right back," Kayla said. She rose and headed into the kitchen.

I looked around and saw the restroom door not far away. I stood, swayed, and caught my balance. Unsteady, I tried to walk unassisted, but my legs seemed weak, and my motor function seemed off. I needed to move slowly from booth to booth until I reached the men's room door. I pulled it open and lunged for the sink. There, I glanced in the mirror. I resembled a raccoon with not one, but two, black eyes. I turned my head and saw a knot at the back of my skull large enough to wear its own hat. Almost too afraid to look, I took a step back and lifted my shirt. My entire torso looked like one giant bruise, and on my left side, I saw a four-inch strip of dirty tape. I assumed Kayla had stitched me up, but I didn't mess with it any further.

The urge to use the facilities struck me, so I hobbled to the toilet, undid my pants, shoved them down, and sat to urinate. As I did, I got an intense stinging sensation. When I finished my business, I stood and pulled up in my pants. When I looked into the toilet, I noticed I had filled it with blood. Somehow, it didn't surprise me.

When I opened the door, Kayla was outside waiting for me.

"Everything okay?" she asked as she reached for my arm to steady me.

"Fine. I just had to pee."

Kayla led me back to my chair, and I sat down, glad to be off my feet. She unscrewed the top off of the bottle of soda and held it out for me. I reached for it and missed.

"Oh, no," she said.

"What?"

"Do you have double vision, or blurriness, Baker?"

I nodded. "A little bit of both, actually."

"What else?"

I rattled off the rest of my symptoms. Headache. Nausea. Couldn't walk much. I held nothing back except the bloody urine, since there was nothing we could do about that.

"I think you have a concussion," she said.

"Yeah, I think you're right."

She shook her head and moved the bottle to my lips and held it while I drank. It was orange and delicious, whatever it was.

"Well, now what?" she said.

"Good question," I said.

CHAPTER NINETEEN

I fully intended to plan out our next steps with Kayla, but the mere act of drinking half a bottle of orange soda wore me out. Kayla moved a table away and pushed two booths together to create a makeshift bed that I couldn't roll out of. She helped me lie down, and I closed my eyes for a minute.

When I opened them again, the sun had set, and the restaurant was dark and quiet. I struggled to sit, but eventually I pulled myself up and looked around.

"Kayla?"

"I'm here, Baker. How are you doing?"

"I'm not sure. My head hurts and I'm thirsty."

I sensed Kayla moving about and a moment later, a small lantern lit up. Kayla set it on the floor and handed me the orange soda I hadn't finished.

"Sorry, I couldn't find any water. I found these, though." Kayla handed me a snack-sized bag of corn chips. "They're a little stale. Are you hungry?"

A valid question. By all rights I should be since I couldn't remember when I last ate, but my stomach didn't growl, and I didn't detect any other signs of hunger. But, in the new world, if food was scarce, it was better to eat than not. I took the bag and when I couldn't open it, Kayla took it, opened it, and handed it back. Stale was an understatement to describe the snack, but food was food, and the salt made my tongue seem alive. I slowly ate the chips, one at a time, and drank the orange soda.

"How long was I asleep?"

"Long enough for me to go scrounging for supplies. Before you ask, I didn't find much."

"Any chance you found a luxury car with a nice plush leather interior and a doctor inside?" I asked.

Kayla smiled. In the dim light, she brightened the room. She had the best smile of anyone I'd ever known.

"Sorry, man. I tried, though. I don't enjoy the thought of dragging you across the country on my makeshift sled. Do you think you can walk?"

"Let's find out," I said, trying to sound confident, even though I felt less than.

I shuffled another few inches to the end of the booth and placed my feet on the floor. Using the tops of the seats for leverage, I pushed myself to a standing position. Dizziness hit me like a summer afternoon thunderstorm. I tipped forward, flailed my arms for anything to grab on to, and feared falling over.

"Whoa, there," Kayla said as she put her hand on my chest and gently pushed me backward. My legs hit the booth, and I sat. "Okay. That wasn't too bad. We can try again later. How's your vision?"

"I can't tell. It's too dark."

Kayla grabbed the lantern and set it on the booth's back. She moved a chair closer and sat in front of me.

"Can you see me?" she asked.

"Of course."

"Okay, how many fingers am I holding up?"

Kayla flashed me the peace sign.

"Two."

She skipped through the motions, putting up random numbers of digits in a quick sequence, only giving me a second to answer before moving onto the next one. When she seemed satisfied that I wasn't completely blind, she stopped.

"Okay, now keep your head straight ahead and follow my finger," she ordered.

I did as instructed and kept my focus on her finger as she moved it back and forth in front of my face.

"You know what you're looking for?" I asked.

"Nah, I caught this on a TV show once and have always wanted to try it. Now hush and do it again."

Kayla repeated the exercise and dropped her hand and crinkled her nose, which was never a good sign.

"What's up?" I asked.

"Your right eye isn't tracking as smooth as the left. Can you see okay out of it?"

I closed my left eye and looked around with my right. "Seems a little blurry, but I can't tell for sure."

"Hold on," Kayla said. She left and returned in a moment with a menu.

"Can you read this?"

I took it and focused on the menu with my right eye only, then switched to my left. "I'll take the burrito. No guacamole, though. That's gross."

Kayla glared at me.

"Okay, my right eye is a wee bit blurry. But, on the positive side, my double vision is gone. Speaking of gone, have those men been back around?"

Kayla took the menu from me, set it to the side, and sat back in her chair. "Yeah. They came back about an hour after we settled in here. I think they know we're around here somewhere, but luckily, they haven't found us yet. They left after the sun set, so I hope we'll be fine here until the morning."

"Maybe we should get out of here. Hit the road," I suggested.

"How? I can't find a car, and you can't walk. We'd be two fish on the highway if I had to pull you down the interstate."

I didn't reply. She was right.

"Okay. How about this? Let's switch places. You get some sleep and I'll stand guard. In the morning, we can figure out the next move."

Kayla considered it for a moment, then helped me get settled into her chair, and she took my place in the booth. By the time I'd shifted my butt enough to get comfortable, Kayla was already breathing deep and on her way to dreamland.

I'd like to say that I stayed alert until the sun rose, but that would be an outright lie. Although, to my credit, I didn't exactly sleep, either. I dozed, immediately awake, every time I heard a sound. The first was from the roof, like something had dropped there, and the others were soft squeaks and shuffling feet, so I assumed we shared the space with a mouse or two.

When the sky brightened, I stood with some effort and took some tentative steps. I was still unsteady and had trouble with my coordination, so although it wasn't the smartest idea in the world, I made sure I'd set the safety on the rifle and used it as a cane. I needed to pee, but I didn't want to use the men's room. Instead, I found my way to the back door, opened it, and used the rifle to prop it open. I felt well enough to stand, and did so, relieving myself against the building. When I finished, I looked down at the little puddle I'd made and gave a sigh of relief when I saw my urine wasn't as red as the day before. I lifted my shirt to check the bandage and found it red, damp, and sticky. I'd need Kayla to look at it. Finished, I hobbled my way back into the building. As I did, I spotted movement out the front window. An old blue Chevy drove by at no more than five miles an hour. The leader of the pack was behind the wheel, still wearing the denim jacket.

"Kayla, wake up," I said.

She jumped up at once. "What?"

I nodded toward the front window. "Company out front."

"How many?"

"I only saw one in the car."

"That's what they were doing last night. One was driving around while the others checked the buildings."

I moved farther down the window and looked out. Sure enough, the men on foot were going from place to place, presumably looking for us.

"What should we do?" Kayla asked.

"Well, I can't run away, so I guess I'm sticking here and if they come this way, I'll fight them off the best I can," I said. "You should go. Head out the back door and leave. I'll cover your escape."

"Uh-uh. No way. I'm staying here with you."

I nodded. "Good. Do you want the rifle or the handgun?"

"I'll take the rifle. You wouldn't be able to hit anything at any distance with that vision."

I handed Kayla the rifle, and she rummaged through the backpack until she found the gun and ammo we had in there.

"You sure you can handle that thing?" I asked.

Kayla looked at me and smiled. "Oh, bless your heart. I'm from Texas. Of course I can."

She took a position near the front door, and I settled into a booth near the window. We watched as the car came around again and slowly passed by.

"He's doing circles," Kayla said.

"Yeah, so?"

"You see where his buddies went?"

I moved down the window until I had a better view of the street. "They're a couple of blocks back. There's a strip mall there that all three are going to."

"Okay. I have a plan," Kayla said.

"What?"

"I take out the driver the next time he comes past, then we run out, steal his car, and boogie on out of here."

"Think you can hit him?" I asked.

"Sure thing. I'm more concerned that we won't have enough time to make it to the car once his buddies hear the shot."

"How far do you think it is to the road?"

"We'll probably have to cover sixty or seventy feet. Are you up for that?" she asked.

"I guess I'll have to be."

"Okay. Get ready."

Kayla unlocked the door, opened it a crack, and slipped the muzzle outside. While she did that, I gathered everything back up into the backpack and put it on. That simple action caused pain to run through my entire torso, but I breathed through the pain and readied myself.

"He's coming," Kayla said.

I hobbled to the door and took up a position behind her so I could be out the door at the same time as she was. The car came closer. Kayla stiffened, and she didn't move except for her breathing and her trigger finger as she moved into position. When the Chevy lined up with us, she pulled the trigger. I saw a hole appear in the driver's window and the car stopped and then it turned and slowly drifted in our direction until it came to rest when it hit a telephone pole.

The door opened and a second later; the man stepped out, holding his neck, blood pouring between his fingers. His mouth opened and closed twice like a carp and fell.

"Come on," Kayla said.

When she got out the door, she waited for me. I put my arm around her and she half-carried, half-dragged me to the car. She pushed me into the passenger seat, got behind the wheel, and threw it in Reverse. Something hit the back window, and I looked behind us in time to see the second bullet further star the glass. The three men were running up the street, taking random potshots at us as they did.

"Punch it," I said.

Kayla did and laid rubber on the street as she sped up. Within a minute, we were back on the interstate and headed east.

"How much gas do we have?" I asked.

Kayla checked the gauge. "Over half a tank. Should get us all the way to Chattanooga."

"We can't take the interstate there. The bridge is out over the river. We'll need to take a couple of state highways to get around. I'll plot out the route."

As I struggled out of the backpack, my shirt lifted a bit.

"Oh, shit, Baker, you're bleeding."

I looked down and saw the bandage saturated with my blood. I watched as a drop escaped and trailed down my stomach.

"Damn," I said.

"Here. Hold these on there."

Kayla thrust a handful of fast-food napkins into my hand. I didn't ask where she got them from, but a quick glance told me they were at least clean. I held them tight over my wound and pressed hard until I thought I'd pass out from the pain.

"We need to find a place to pull over and look at that," Kayla said. "Are there any towns up ahead? Preferably one with a clinic or a hospital. Or a sporting goods store. Or a pharmacy?"

I fumbled with the pack, opening it with one hand, then I removed the contents, throwing them to the floor by my feet until I finally found the map of Alabama. I struggled to open it and found our approximate location on the map, then, out of habit, traced the route with the index finger on my left hand. As I did, it left a red smear behind on the map.

"Our best bet is probably Gadsden. That's about an hour from here."

"You think you can hold on until then?" Kayla asked.

"I hope so."

Kayla punched the accelerator to the floor, and at first, I watched as the speedometer needle climbed higher and higher, then I leaned back, held the napkins as tight as I could, and watched the landscape as it raced by.

Almost an hour later, I spotted the sign leading us to the town of Gadsden, and Kayla took the exit without slowing. It wasn't until she'd almost made it all the way down the ramp that she realized she was going too fast and stepped on the brake. We both lurched forward, lucky we'd both put on our seatbelts.

"Sorry," she said. "Which way?"

I spotted a blue sign with a capital letter H on it, the sign for a hospital, and pointed toward the arrow. Kayla followed the signs until at last we found a three-story, red-bricked hospital. Kayla pulled right up to the emergency room door and parked the car. There was a wheelchair right next to the door, so Kayla pulled it next to the car and helped me get in. The doors opened when we neared, and she wheeled me right into the hospital.

"Whoa, there."

Kayla stopped in her tracks when she heard the voice. We looked over and saw someone sitting behind the receptionist's desk wearing a white jacket and reading a magazine.

"We don't want any trouble. My friend got hurt and I need to patch him up, then we'll leave," Kayla said.

The man behind the desk stood up. "You'll get no trouble from me. In fact, I can help you. Folks around here call me Doc Patrick."

"We have no money to pay you," I said.

"That's good because there's nowhere to spend it. I deal in trade."

"What do you want?" Kayla asked.

The doctor stepped around the counter and took control of the wheelchair. "We'll worry about that later. Come on."

Kayla followed behind as the doctor wheeled me into the first examination room we came to. While he slipped into some sterile gloves, Kayla helped me onto the table and got my shirt off of me.

"Let's see what we have here." The doctor removed the bandage and washed down the area with saline. My three-inch wound looked horrible, crudely stitched with what looked like regular sewing thread. The lines were jagged and angry red. "What happened here?"

"I got stabbed."

"Who did this?"

"I did. I had to use what I had on hand. He wouldn't stop bleeding," Kayla said.

"Not the best field dressing I've seen come through here in the last couple of years. Not the worst, either. I'm going to have to take this apart and suture it so it will heal properly. And you've got an infection starting up in here. Are you allergic to anything? Penicillin or anything else?"

I shook my head. "No."

"Good." The doctor stepped from the room and returned a minute later with a hypodermic needle and two vials. He tapped into the first one and jabbed it into my belly without warning. "That will take the edge off."

The doc waited a minute, then pressed around my wound. "Feel that?"

"No."

"Good. This is penicillin. Should take care of the immediate problem, and before you leave here, I'll rustle up some pills for you."

I leaned back on the table and let the doctor go to work. He injected the antibiotic first, then went to work removing the crude stitches Kayla had given me, then added his own. When he was done, he swabbed me down with a bronze-colored solution and put on a fresh bandage.

"That should do the trick. You can get up and dressed. Be right back with your meds."

Kayla helped me sit up, then got me back into my shirt. When the doctor returned with my pills, she told him about the possible concussion I had. Since he had no other patients, the doctor gave me as thorough an examination as he could, declared I did have a slight concussion, and since there was nothing he could do about it, suggested I get as much rest as possible. He also mentioned that although I was badly beaten, he didn't think I had any broken bones or internal bleeding. Hooray for me.

Kayla got me back in the wheelchair and pushed me out to the car. I waited in the shade while she and the doctor discussed the fee. He shook his head at everything Kayla offered from our stash, then got excited when she opened the trunk, and he looked in the back. Kayla stepped back and gave me a thumbs up, and once the doc finished rummaging around and had taken what he wanted, he closed the trunk then helped me get settled in the passenger seat.

"Oh, here," the doc said as he pulled a bottle of pills from his pocket. "Almost forgot to give these to you. Take one of these twice a day, starting today. Take two tonight, then one in the morning and one at night. There's about twelve days of pills in there. Finish them all. And only drink water that you've boiled, purified, or bottled. Got it?"

I nodded. "Thanks, Doc."

"Oh, shit. Wait here a moment."

We weren't in a big hurry, so we sat patiently in the car. Five minutes later, the doc appeared and handed me a cane through the passenger window.

"Use this until you get your strength back."

"Thanks again, Doc," I said.

Doc Patrick waved, then ambled back into the hospital, stopping to pick up one box he'd taken from us.

"What did you give him?" I asked as I watched him step through the door.

"No clue. I never looked in the trunk. Let's get out of here," Kayla said.

CHAPTER TWENTY

Kayla kept us on Highway 11 so we wouldn't have to backtrack later to avoid the bridge out over the Tennessee River. We made it another hour to the town of Fort Payne, and as we passed the only church in town, the car sputtered, the engine died, and Kayla coasted off the road and into the parking lot.

"Well, so much for getting as far as Chattanooga," I said.

"We're out of gas. All we need to do is find a station and we'll be back up and running," Kayla answered.

"If I'm not mistaken, there's one about a half of a mile up the road," I said.

"Okay. You wait here with the car, and I'll go get gas. I should be back in a half an hour or so."

"I could come with you," I offered.

"You're going to walk a mile round trip?" Kayla eyed me in disbelief.

"I can do it."

Kayla got out of the car, walked around to my side, and opened my door.

"Okay, mister. Get your cane and give it a try. You would surprise me if you could make ten feet, let alone the fifty-two hundred it would take for a mile."

She'd thrown down the challenge, but I thought I was up for the journey, so I swung my legs out and grabbed my cane. Kayla put out a hand to help me from the car, but I pushed it away and lifted myself up, using the door instead. I put the cane in front of me and took a step. I needed to will my body to follow it and once I took that step, I immediately regretted it. My stomach felt like I'd gotten stabbed all over again, my legs were so unsteady I started to shake, and a sweat broke out on my forehead. This time, when Kayla offered her hand, I swallowed my pride and let her guide me back to my seat.

"Okay, how about I wait here in the car, and you go for gas?" I said.

Kayla gave me a smile. "Baker, that's an excellent plan."

"I don't suppose there's a gas can in the car?"

Kayla looked in the back seat and opened the trunk and checked in there. "Nope. Hopefully, I'll find one at the station."

"Take the backpack with you. It would be easier to carry in there. And don't forget the rifle."

Kayla nodded. She emptied the backpack onto her seat and grabbed the rifle. "I'll see if I can find you some water to take your pills with."

Without another word, Kayla headed up the road, and I watched her until she was out of sight. Then I tried to get comfortable in the car. I rolled down all the windows to let the breeze in, and when that wasn't enough, I opened all the doors.

Finally comfortable, I dozed. Somewhere in my dreams, I heard a rousing rendition of *Amazing Grace* being sung, and it got louder as my dream passed on. Wanting the song to end, I opened my eyes and discovered it wasn't a dream at all. There, directly in front of the car, was a man dressed in black preacher's robes with long brown hair that reminded me of Jesus. Behind him marched fifteen or twenty people, all singing *Amazing Grace*, and all headed right toward me. The preacher stopped right next to me, but the song continued until the verse finished and the preacher put a fist in the air to end the tune.

The preacher dropped his fist and raised his other hand in which was a Bible the same color as his robes. "And, lo, I traveled across the desert and there I met a stranger who God sent as an emissary to answer my prayers. What is your name, stranger?"

It took a moment to register that he was speaking to me. "Baker."

"Baker what?"

"Nothing. Only Baker."

The preacher turned around to address the congregation. "Friends, we've long prayed for a miracle, and the Lord has sent us Baker. Like when Jesus multiplied the loaves to feed those at the Sea of Galilee, another baker will perform a miracle."

"You must have me confused with someone else. I'm not a miracle worker," I argued.

"Ah, but you are. When we headed out for our walk this morning, we prayed for a vehicle, and we return and you've delivered one to our doorstep."

"Oh, no. There's a misunderstanding. We ran out of gas here. My friend went to get some."

"There's a misunderstanding, son, but it's yours. It's no coincidence that you ran out of gas here. It was God's will!"

"God's will!" the congregation repeated.

"You don't get it. My friend will return soon, and shortly after that, we'll be out of your parking lot and on our way."

I made a move to close the door, but the preacher stepped in front of it so I couldn't achieve my goal. "Would you mind stepping back, sir?"

He leaned forward and laughed in my face. "Step back? No, Mr. Baker. You're on God's land here, and we are his children. We won't step back. Perhaps you should step away."

"Although I'd love to, I've had an accident and can't walk," I said, holding up my cane for effect.

"Do you believe in Jesus?" the preacher asked.

"Uh," I started.

"Jesus believes in you! Lord Jesus will make you walk! Jesus will heal you! Heed my words and rise and walk!"

"Rise and walk! Rise and walk!" the congregation chanted.

"I'm not quite sure that's the way it works," I said.

"Son, I'm getting the idea that you're not quite the man of God you think you are. Now, are you going to make an offering to the Lord's house?" the preacher asked.

"I'd prefer it if you just left me in peace. Like I said, my friend will be back soon. Then we'll be on our way."

"Deacons, come and collect this man's offering," the preacher said, ignoring me.

At that point, I'd had enough and brought out the gun I'd been hiding and hoping I wouldn't have to use.

"Please step away from the car," I ordered.

A grimace passed over the preacher's face, and he raised his hands in the air. "You dare pull a gun on one of God's servants?"

"Step away and we'll be out of your hair in a bit."

The preacher lowered his hands and swung the Bible. It hit the side of the 9mm and pushed my forearm into the door frame. I lost my grip, and the gun clattered onto the pavement.

"Deacons. The offerings."

The preacher stepped aside, and two large black men, wearing matching black suits and white ties, stepped into view. One leaned into the car and plucked me from the seat like I was a five-pound bag of flour. Once out of the car, the two men dragged me several yards from the car, then unceremoniously dropped me on my butt onto the scalding asphalt of the parking lot. I tried to get up, but one man held his hand on my shoulder, keeping me pinned to the ground.

Unable to do anything, I watched as the preacher stepped away from the car and several members of the congregation stepped in to ransack the vehicle like locusts from the eighth plague. Any item deemed of no value they flung from the car, including my maps, the pine tree air freshener that was attached to the rear-view mirror, and another stack of fast-food napkins that fluttered to the ground like dying kites.

After a few minutes, the doors all closed except the driver's. A dainty white woman in a yellow sundress appeared with a five-gallon gas can she struggled with until a man in overalls took it from her and used it to fill the empty tank while the woman got behind the wheel. Once filled, the man put the can in the trunk, gave a hand signal, and the woman drove the blue Chevy away.

Once the car was out of sight, the congregation headed toward the church and disappeared inside. A shadow fell over me, and I looked up and saw the preacher standing before me with my cane. He handed me the cane and smiled.

"The Lord thanks you for your generosity."

The deacon holding me down let me go, and the two men headed for the church without so much as an invitation for me to join them.

I sat on the blistering concrete for a few minutes, then got to my knees, and with the help of the cane, got to my feet. I hobbled over to the litter in the parking lot, and from it collected my road maps, which were the only thing of value to me left in the pile. They'd driven off with the rest of the items Kayla had put in the car when she emptied the backpack, including the few survival supplies we had, our satellite phones, all of Kayla's stuff, and the extra ammo. I looked around for my gun, but that was gone, too. I was lucky I'd stashed the pills the doctor had given me in my pocket and that they hadn't bothered to search me.

Not wanting to hang around the church, I crossed the street and lumbered down the road. My pace seemed slow because it was. Minute after minute ticked by, and every time I turned around, I could still see the church's steeple. When it at last slipped from view, I spotted a large tree ahead and angled for it. Once there, I collapsed on the grass underneath the shade. I was sweating profusely, my body ached, and I didn't think I could manage another step. In all, I'd traveled about three blocks at an average speed of a block every seven minutes.

I waited with my back to the tree, and ten minutes later, Kayla appeared on the other side of the street. She must have been deep in thought because she never saw me, and it wasn't until I whistled at her she noticed me, crossed the highway, and joined me under the tree.

"What are you doing here? Why aren't you with the car?" she asked when she got close enough.

"Would you believe I got carjacked by a preacher?"

"No shit?"

I nodded.

"Damn. Not cool. Especially considering all the trouble we experienced in stealing it in the first place."

Kayla placed the backpack on the ground and sat. "Are you okay? You don't look well."

"I thought it best to get away from there. You find any gas?"

Kayla opened the backpack and dumped out the contents. "Plenty of gas, but all I found was this for a container." She pointed at an old two-liter bottle filled with an amber colored liquid. There were several mini bottles of water on the ground, and she took one, opened it, and handed it to me.

"Drink," she said. "I also have a treat for us."

From her pocket, she extracted a Twix bar. She opened the chocolate and gave me half of it. It was a little stale and partially melted, but still delicious. When I finished it, I licked my fingers clean and drank the water.

"What next?" I asked.

Kayla thought for a minute, then sighed. "Well, either I venture off by myself and try to find another vehicle, or we keep heading north and hope we come across a new ride. Or we can find someplace to hold up until you're able to move better. Maybe we can at least find some bikes."

"Let's keep moving," I said. "I'd like to get out of this town as soon as possible. I'll push myself as much as I can."

"No, you won't. Let's take it easy. When you need a break, we'll stop. We're in no hurry."

We sat for a few more minutes, then Kayla helped me to my feet and we resumed our journey. It hurt like hell, but I pushed on, slowly at first, then slower when I quickly tired and the pain in my abdomen became my primary focus. We would walk for ten minutes before Kayla would force me to sit and rest for a while. Eventually, the ten minutes became seven, and that shortened to five. After one final push and lots of encouragement, we at last made it to the gas station and convenience store from which Kayla had retrieved the gas hours before. The inside of the store was gutted, but Kayla found a folding chair behind the counter for me to sit on. She let me rest while she explored the property.

A few minutes later, she popped back into the store and grinned at me. "Come on outside. I found the solution to our problem."

I followed her out the door and looked at what she'd found.

"What's that?" I asked.

"It's a cart thing. I found it in the storage room." I looked over the large blue plastic bin. It stood about three feet high and long, and a couple of feet wide.

"What are we supposed to do with that?" I asked.

"You get in, and I push it. At least until we find something better."

"You want me to lie in there like I'm a pile of laundry, and you're going to push me up the highway in it?"

Kayla smiled and nodded.

"No way. I couldn't fit in there, and if I did, I'd be so uncomfortable I wouldn't be able to stand it for long."

Kayla looked at me, then at the bin. She snapped her fingers, then headed into the store and came back with the folding chair. She placed it inside the bin. It just fit and left enough room in there for me.

"Get in," she said.

It took some effort and Kayla's help, but I got into the bin and sat on the chair.

"I look ridiculous," I said.

"Yeah, but how's the comfort?" she asked.

"Not too bad," I admitted.

"Okay, hold on. Here we go."

Kayla took off the pack and put it in the bin with me and handed me the rifle. She got behind me, and with a grunt and a big push, we were rolling. She pushed me without complaint along that Alabama highway for two hours, and when she couldn't go anymore, we found a small, abandoned farmhouse. The driveway was stone, so Kayla helped me out of the cart and guided me to the door. We broke in and bunked down for the night.

The next morning, I woke with sunlight streaming through the window and onto my face.

"Kayla?"

A moment later, she appeared with a bottle of water and a plastic bowl full of cherries.

"Do you like fresh cherries?" she asked.

"I do. Do you?"

"I love them. There was a tree out back, so get ready for a great breakfast."

She joined me on the couch and handed me the water. "Take your antibiotic."

Without arguing, I complied as she started in on the cherries. Once I'd washed down the pill, I joined her. I put a cherry in my mouth, then careful to avoid the pit, I bit to the side of it. I rolled my eyes when the juice exploded from the fruit. Carefully, I turned the cherry in my mouth, ate around the pit, then spit the pit into my hand.

"Okay. That's gross," Kayla said.

"How are you supposed to eat a cherry?" I asked.

"Like this."

Kayla selected a cherry from the bowl, held it with two fingers, then nibbled her way around the fruit like a squirrel might do. When she finished, she held the pit up for me to see.

"You still have flesh on there," I argued. "My way is more efficient."

"But what will you do with your pit?" she asked.

"Don't know. What are you going to do with yours? It seems we had different techniques but ended up with the same problem."

"Hold this." Without waiting for an answer, Kayla dropped her pit in my palm, went to the kitchen, and returned with a gravy boat etched with a cornucopia on the side.

"Fancy." I said as I dropped both pits into the boat.

Together, we attacked the bowl of cherries and quickly emptied the contents.

"How are you feeling?" Kayla asked.

"About the same as yesterday, except I'm stiff from sleeping on this couch all night."

"We could stay here for a few days until you're feeling better. Would you be up for that?"

"To be honest, I'd like to go. I'm tired of being on the road, and I'd like to be at home sleeping in my own bed. But since you have to do all the hard work, I'm going to leave it up to you."

"Okay, Baker. I'm going to go refill this bowl, so we have a snack while on the road. Why don't you scavenge around the house and see if there's anything useful for us?"

Kayla left the house and left me to wander around. My first stop was to the bathroom where I used the facilities. It pleased me to see my urine had no trace of blood in it, although I could tell by the smell and color that I needed more water. Afterward, I explored from room to room looking for things to take with us. I found a couple of pillows and extra pillowcases to use as sacks. In the bathroom I found a fully stocked medicine cabinet and from there selected a full bottle of aspirin, a bottle of multi-vitamins, and a tube of cinnamon-flavored toothpaste still in its box. I threw all those items in a pillowcase and moved on to the next room. In the main bedroom, I found three men's shirts that could fit either of us, and an unopened package of men's socks.

By the time I made it back to the living room, there were two Tupperware bowls with covers filled with cherries. Next to those was a gallon-sized plastic bag filled with cutlery, a manual can opener, three plastic cups, a small cooking pot with a lid, and a metal teapot. Everything except the bowls of cherries I loaded into one of the empty pillowcases. Then I sat on the couch and waited for Kayla.

She surprised me when she entered from the front door and not the rear.

"You ready? I've got a big surprise for you."

"Yeah, I'm ready." I grabbed my cane and one pillowcase. Kayla grabbed the rest, and we left the house.

Kayla surprised me all right. Waiting just outside the front door was a horse hitched to a small wagon.

"Oh, my, he's beautiful," I said. I set my pillowcase down and stepped down from the porch and approached the animal. The horse was chestnut from nose to tail, except for a patch of white on the nose. "Where did you find him?"

"First off, he's a her. There's a barn out in the back forty and she was in her stall."

"Someone took off and just left her here? That's so cruel."

"The doors to the stall and barn were wide open. I expect they set her free, and she just came back. You ready to ride in style?"

I looked at the wagon. "Seems too high for me. I'm not sure I can get up there."

"No problem. I got that covered," Kayla said as she walked to the back. "I think they used this thing for hayrides."

She pulled out a stepladder and set it next to the wagon. She guided me up, and got me settled in the seat, then she returned the ladder to the back and stowed all of our items in the wagon.

Once everything was together, she hopped up and took the reins.

"You sure you can handle this thing?" I asked.

"Of course. Like I said before, I'm from Texas."

CHAPTER TWENTY-ONE

Traveling by horse-drawn wagon wasn't the fastest mode of travel, but it was a pleasant one. The horse was good natured and pulled the wagon without hesitation. We traveled for a few hours and when the road crossed over a stream, Kayla unhitched the horse and gave it time to drink and munch as much grass as it wanted. I decided this was the way to go in the new world. We didn't have to worry about finding gas, oil, or mechanical breakdowns. And, as a bonus, the horse did all the hard work. When the horse was ready, Kayla hooked it back up to the wagon, and we continued on. By the time we stopped for the night, we'd said goodbye to Alabama and Georgia and found a small pasture to bunk down in for the night just north of the Tennessee state line.

While Kayla took care of the horse, I made up a bed for us in the back of the wagon. Using the pillows I'd taken from the house and the blankets that were already in the wagon, we were ready to go. When Kayla returned and hopped into the wagon, she broke out the cherries and we had a snack under the approaching stars.

"We should give her a name," Kayla said.

"How about Lady Clementine?" I suggested.

She thought it over for a second, then shook her head. "No. That doesn't seem right for her."

"What do you think is better? Sally? Athena? Wildflower?"

"No. Those don't work either."

"Storm? Faith? River?"

Kayla dismissed my suggestions.

"I got it! Black Beauty!"

Kayla swung her head to face me. "Seriously, Baker? She's not even black."

"Sorry. I've never been around horses. Never even ridden one, so naming them is a bit of out of my wheelhouse."

Kayla grunted and returned to eating her cherries. I noticed every time she finished one; she put her pit into a plastic baggie while I, on the other hand, had dumped mine over the wagon's side and onto the ground.

"Why are you saving those?" I asked.

"Do you have any cherry trees on your property?"

"No, I don't think so."

"Well, you will after I plant these," she said with a wink.

I didn't know if cherry trees would grow in Virginia, but if she wanted to try it, I figured I could find a place for them.

"Nutmeg. Definitely Nutmeg," Kayla blurted.

"You want to grow nutmeg, too? Okay. Does that come from a tree or a plant? I don't even know. That's a spice, right? For pumpkin pie? I don't grow pumpkins either, since I never cared for them much. If you gave me a slice of pumpkin pie, I'd eat an inch off the tip of the triangle, and that would be my ration for the rest of the year."

"Not the spice. The horse. Her name is Nutmeg," she explained.

"Nutmeg, huh? If that works for you, it works for me."

I decided when we got back home, I'd restock the pasture with as many horses as we could properly care for. Since I knew nothing about the regal animals, I'd need to find another library and checkout some animal husbandry books.

"You good on cherries?" she asked.

I took one more and Kayla closed the container and placed it off to the side. We watched in silence as the stars erupted in the night sky.

"You want me to take the first watch?" she asked.

I thought about the last couple of days we had. She'd taken out the man who bested me and stolen his car. She walked a mile for gas, pushed me for miles in a cart, and at times literally carried or dragged me through two states. And now she wanted the first watch.

"No. Hand me the rifle. I'll take it."

"You sure?"

"Yeah. We're in a pretty remote spot here, so I doubt we'll have any encounters."

She handed me the gun, rolled over onto her side, and slipped off to sleep. As far as I was concerned, she deserved as much rest as she could get, so I planned on not waking her at all and vowed to stand guard myself the entire night.

I heard something beneath the wagon, so I woke, fully alert, and peered over the wagon. A squirrel had sneaked up on us while I was catnapping and was busy gathering the cherry pits I'd tossed on the ground. At that point, I realized I hadn't stayed awake all night, and had dropped off not long after Kayla did. I turned around and looked at her. She was still sleeping on her side, but had pulled the blanket up over her shoulders.

As quietly as I could, I got off the wagon and worked through my morning routine in which I did my morning business, then took my antibiotics and a couple of aspirin. There was no need for me to make breakfast since all we had were the cherries, so I walked a bit to stretch my legs. I was still unsteady and needed the cane, but I felt stronger than I had in the previous days. With a grunt, I lifted my shirt to check the bandage, and saw there was no blood seeping through, and it itched simply to view it. I took those both as good signs.

Nutmeg was twenty yards away munching on some wildflowers, so I approached her slowly, more out of fear of falling, and to a lesser extent so I wouldn't spook her.

"Hey. Hey Nutmeg," I said as I got closer.

She took a single step back, but then held still when I got close enough to pet her neck. In response, she gave me a horse huff, let me stroke her a couple more times, then returned to eating the flowers. I took that as a good sign, too.

"Making friends?" Kayla asked.

"I'm trying too. She seems like a good horse."

"She's the best horse ever!" Kayla said, then laughed. "Can you help me get her hooked up to the wagon?"

"For sure. That's a process I'll need to learn, eventually."

Once Kayla had gone through her morning routine and we'd eaten the remainder of the cherries, it was time to get Nutmeg ready for the day. Kayla took her time explaining the different parts of the bridle and slowly demonstrated putting it on the horse. Once she'd finished that task, she showed me how to attach the horse to the wagon. I wanted to get in there and actually help rather than just have it explained to me, but I still relied on my cane for balance and couldn't do much with just one hand. Once in the wagon, Kayla handed me the reins and instructed me on how to drive the wagon.

There were a few people out on the streets of Chattanooga as we passed through the city, and each person we saw returned our wave with one of their own. I knew it would cost us some time, but I wanted to check in on Collins and his wife.

When we got to his house, I stopped Nutmeg in front of a No Parking sign and waited while Kayla got out of the wagon and set up the stepladder for me. While she tied the reins to the sign, I lumbered up to the front door, rang the bell, and waited. I expected Taylor to make an appearance with her shotgun, but she didn't.

"Anyone home?" Kayla asked when she joined me on the porch.

I rang the bell again, pounded on the door, and waited some more. After a full minute, I repeated my actions. When no one answered, Kayla reached out and turned the knob. The door freely opened, so Kayla pushed it wide and stepped in.

"Hello?" she said to the dark interior.

"Collins? Taylor?" I called out. "It's Baker. I'm here with my friend."

No answer.

"Stay here," I said.

Kayla moved back to the door, and I did a sweep of the rooms. When I crossed the threshold into the kitchen, I stopped without entering. Collins was sitting slumped over at the kitchen table. He faced away from me, which was a blessing because there was a large hole in the back of his head. Taylor lay face down on the floor next to the refrigerator in a similar state. They'd been dead long enough that the expansive blood pool that encompassed half of the tile floor had darkened to a deep maroon. I backtracked to the living room.

"Let's get out of here," I said, pushing Kayla through the door.

"What's going on?"

"They're both dead. We need to leave now."

While I climbed into the wagon, Kayla unhitched Nutmeg, handed me the reins, and a minute later we were off.

For three days, we followed Tennessee Highway 11 northeast. Every little town we came to, we found good-hearted people who were keen on making conversation. It turned out, besides her skills as a good horse, Nutmeg was pretty enough that people seemed compelled to approach us and pet her. One kind soul offered her a handful of sugar cubes, then gave us the remainder of the box to feed her when we felt she deserved a treat.

When we got closer to Knoxville, I got out my Tennessee state map and got my bearings.

"It's over that way," I said, pointing out the direction to Kayla. "There's a barge there that will take us across the river. Is Nutmeg going to be okay on a barge?"

Kayla shrugged. "I guess we're going to find out."

She found the path and steered the wagon down to the riverside. The barge was on the opposite side of the river, but once I got the bargeman's attention, he activated his winch system and crossed the river to us.

"You again?" he said once he'd secured his barge to the shore.

"You remember me?" I asked.

"Sure. You were with the ranger. What was that, ten days? Two weeks ago?"

"We'd like to cross," I said.

"Obviously. What you got to offer?"

"We're not sure the horse will take to the barge," Kayla said. "Can we try getting him on first?"

The bargeman looked from me, to Kayla, to Nutmeg. "I reckon."

We got off the wagon and Kayla walked to Nutmeg and scratched her on the nose. "Come on, girl. We're going to go for a short boat ride, okay? Come on."

Kayla tugged gently on the bridle, imploring Nutmeg to move, but she wouldn't.

"Come on, Nutmeg. It will be okay. I promise."

Kayla tugged again, but the horse didn't move.

"Let me try," I said, joining Kayla.

I held my hand out in front of Nutmeg's nose. She sniffed at me and inched forward a bit. I took a step back, and Nutmeg followed me. When I took another step back, she moved forward again. I repeated the process until I'd walked three quarters of the way across the barge.

"That's good," the bargeman said.

"How did you do that?" Kayla asked.

"Nutmeg and I have a special bond," I said. I held open my hand and let Nutmeg take the two sugar cubes from my palm.

Kayla laughed. "Special bond. That's more like bribery."

"Well, it worked, didn't it?"

"It did," she admitted. "You'd better hold tight to her reins, so she doesn't bolt."

"A-hem."

We both turned around at the sound. The bargeman was standing near the wagon with his arms crossed.

"The horse is on. What you go to trade for a ride?"

"Take a gander in the wagon," I said. "See what we have."

The bargeman climbed up to make a closer inspection and climbed down a minute later. "You got nothing on here I need nor want. Get off my barge."

"Hold her," Kayla said, then moved to the bargeman. "Look, I don't know if you know anything about horses, but they need to be trained to walk backwards, and this one hasn't been. And there's certainly not enough room on the barge to turn her around. So, take us across the river, and we'll pay you what you want when we get to the other side."

The bargeman laughed, then spit over the side. "Listen, lady, I was born at night, but not last night. I ain't falling for that one. Y'all unhitch the horse from the wagon, push the wagon off, then turn the horse around."

"Are you going to help?"

The bargeman sneered. "Nope. Your problem. Not mine."

"Look, my friend over there got hurt. He can barely walk. He couldn't help me push this heavy wagon."

The bargeman shrugged. "Again. Not my problem."

Both stopped speaking, and I figured we were in the middle of a stalemate.

"Look," Kayla said, dropping the tone of her voice and adding a side of softness. "Surely we can work out a deal of some kind."

She pushed her hair away from her face in a drawn-out move and stuck out her chest. Her posture surprised me, but then I realized she was digging out yet another tool from her arsenal: sex appeal. It was a strange transition for me. Over the last few days, I'd come to see Kayla as a fierce warrior, like an Amazon. I got used to seeing her with dirt on her face, and her hair messy, and her clothes muddy. But now, standing there in the morning sun with the light shining through her blond hair, I realized how beautiful she was. Even more so than the day I first met her.

"Kayla," I said. When I spoke, I let go of the reins, and Nutmeg immediately whinnied and moved. I reached for the reins and secured the horse.

"I got this, Baker."

She turned her attention back to the bargeman. "You want to work out a deal or not?"

The bargeman stepped forward and put a dirty hand on her shoulder. "I think we can come to some terms."

"Then get us moving and let's get down to business," Kayla said.

The bargeman went to the winch, slipped it into the correct gear, and turned it on. There must have been a slow setting, because although we moved, we did so at my current walking pace. Once we were moving, he returned to Kayla.

"Here's what's gonna happen. You're going to get on your knees and take care of me until I'm satisfied."

"Kayla, no!" I yelled.

From inside his cruddy overalls, the bargeman produced a pistol. I looked up and saw the rifle leaning on the wagon seat, right in the middle between where Kayla and I usually sat.

"Knees. Now," he said, leveling the gun at Kayla's head.

Kayla looked at me, then complied.

The bargeman unclipped one strap of his overalls and then the other.

"Pull them down," he ordered.

Kayla gripped the overalls at each hip and worked them down until they were in a pile at his feet.

"Kayla, don't do it," I said.

"Just take care of Nutmeg. Make sure she doesn't get riled." Kayla winked at me and turned her attention back to the bargeman when he pressed the muzzle of the gun against her head.

"Take care of business, bitch," he grunted.

At that moment, I loosened my grip on the reins and blew hard into Nutmeg's nose. In response, the horse whinnied again and took a step backwards to get away from me. The wagon moved half a foot, which took the bargeman's attention away from Kayla for a second.

That second was enough. Kayla rose like a linebacker and threw the full bulk of her body into the bargeman. He tried to maintain his footing, got tripped up by his own pants, and fell into the river.

"Whoa, girl," I said, securing the reins. Once Nutmeg was back under control, I looked into the river. I half expected the bargeman to shoot at us, but with his legs trapped in his pants, he had enough trouble trying to keep his head above water. Over the next few seconds, I watched as the current grabbed him and took him for a ride on the Tennessee River.

"Are you okay?" I asked.

"Baker, I'm fine. I'm going to see if I can speed this thing up a bit."

Kayla crossed over to the winch, and a second later we started cutting through the river at a faster clip. When we were twenty feet from the bank, she slowed us down again, and a few seconds later, we contacted the land.

Offloading Nutmeg was a lot easier than loading her because she wanted nothing more than to get off the barge, and she practically pulled me along with her. Once Nutmeg and the wagon were on land, Kayla went through the bargeman's possessions on the barge and added to our supplies some fishing gear, three bottles of water, and a plastic bag filled with strawberries.

As Kayla encouraged Nutmeg to pull us up the boat ramp to the road, I watched her. Although she wore a fierce look of determination on her face, her eyes contained the same soft sparkle I'd remembered from so long ago.

"What? Why are you staring at me?" she asked.

"I think you're amazing," I said. "And beautiful."

She laughed. "Sure, sure. I'm not either one, so what were you really thinking?"

That was another Kayla trademark that I'd remembered from long ago. She sucked at taking genuine compliments, which in a way broke my heart since I'd never said an insincere word to her in all the years I'd known her.

"We should find you a hat. You're getting a sunburn."

CHAPTER TWENTY-TWO

It took us five days to make the trip from Knoxville to Virginia. Over that time, we settled into a routine. Throughout the day, as we counted down the miles, we tended to Nutmeg, scavenged for food and supplies for ourselves, and talked. I did my best to describe my place, my dreams for making it better, and did my best to let Kayla know that since it was her place now, too, she could accept or reject any or all of my proposals.

The most important part of the journey was that as the days passed, I grew stronger. After the second day, my blurry vision cleared up. It wasn't a hundred percent, but I was now at the point where I could tell the difference between a person and a tree at farther than thirty yards. The third day, I finally felt strong and steady enough to move around without the cane. My muscles still had some stiffness in them, but I worked through those by walking alongside Nutmeg for small stretches at a time.

On day four, we found a fully stocked medic's kit inside an abandoned ambulance. Inside were several items, but of most interest to me were the sterile gauze pads and tape to apply them. When we settled in for the night, I sat back while Kayla removed the dressing the doctor had applied. I expected the stitches to look big and clumsy like when Dr. Frankenstein put his monster together, but instead they looked perfectly spaced, each tied into a little knot. The area around the wound had returned to my skin's normal color, so I assumed the antibiotics had done the trick. Kayla suggested we leave the stiches in until we got home, so she smeared them with a topical antibiotic and covered them with a fresh gauze pad.

My heart lifted when I spotted the highway sign that was a few hundred yards from my driveway. My spirits lifted too, and I could have jumped out of the wagon and carried Kayla and Nutmeg the rest of the way, only based on the amount of joy I felt to be finally home.

"The road's a little rough, so we'll have to go slow up the driveway," I said to Kayla. "When we make the turn, you'll have to stop. I'll need to get out and move the tree."

"A tree?" she asked.

"Yeah. We keep it across the driveway to discourage unwanted visitors. It's on a pulley system, so it will take me only a minute to get it out of the way."

Kayla nodded, turned in where I told her, and stopped.

"Wait, this isn't right," I said.

"What?" she asked.

I jumped down from the wagon and walked eight feet up the driveway where the tree should have been. Spotting something on the ground, I squatted and ran my fingers through a shallow pile of sawdust. I looked over at the side of the lane, and sure enough, the large tree trunk we used as a diversion was cut up into multiple pieces and pushed out of the way.

"Stay here with Nutmeg," I said when I returned to the wagon. I retrieved the rifle from the wagon and checked the magazine. I had only three cartridges left, but they'd have to do.

"Baker, what's going on?" Kayla asked.

"I'm not sure yet, but something is wrong. Please, stay here. I'll be back within a half hour."

"You sure?"

"Yeah. In fact, don't stay here. Up the road that way is a small roadside picnic area. I'll meet you up there. It's not far, a tenth of a mile at the most."

Kayla stared at me without moving or speaking.

"Go. Please. I'll be there in a bit."

Without a word, she gave Nutmeg a flip of the reins, and they were on their way.

After they moved up the road, I started my walk up the driveway. I stayed at the center, working hard to avoid any leaves or brittle branches that would give away my footfalls. When I got to the junction where I needed to decide whether to go into the valley to my place, or up the mountain to check on Pops, I gave it a minute's thought and turned right to ascend the mountain.

When the house came into view, I expected Frank and Dino to come running up, and I hoped that they'd remembered me and threatened to kill me with licks instead of mauling me to pieces. Neither dog appeared. I moved closer to the house, stepped to the door, and pushed. It didn't budge.

I rapped on the wood. "Pops? It's me, Baker. Pops? You there?"

There was no answer. Not even the dogs barked. I went to the windows but couldn't see through the curtains. Slowly, I made my way around the house, peeking into each window as I did. In each case, Pops had drawn the curtains, and I couldn't look inside. When I arrived at the rear, the window was open.

"Pops? You in there?" I said.

"Baker?"

"Yeah. It's me."

A set of keys flew out the window and landed at my feet. Taking that as an invitation, I moved back to the front door, let myself in, and made my way to the bedroom.

"Holy shit, Pops, what happened?"

Pops laid in bed with his white shirt covered in dried blood. Tins of old food littered the floor, and the room smelled of spoiled meat, body odor, and human waste.

"We got squatters. Showed up about a week ago. I held them off here, but they moved in on your place."

"How many?"

"Water?" Pops lifted his arm and pointed to the dresser. On it was a pail filled with water. I scooped out a cup and gave it to him. Once he'd wet his whistle, he seemed a little more alert.

"I don't know how many. At least eight. I killed two myself. Afterward they dragged them bodies off and came back. When I barricaded myself in, they put a guard on me. He still there?"

I shook my head. "I didn't notice anyone. Where are Frank and Dino?"

"I don't know. They ran off when the shooting started."

"Can you get up?"

"No, son, I'm spent. I'm surprised I lasted this long. But I'll tell you this, you want your land back, you're going to have to fight for it. Be careful though, these are bad people. I found out they were killing folks in town, and I thought they'd never find us here, but I was wrong."

"I don't have enough ammo," I said.

Pops struggled to smile but managed one. "I got that covered. Go into the outhouse and lift the lid. Underneath you'll find a switch. Flip it to the left and pull up on the handle. You'll know what to do from there."

"What..."

"Baker, get going. You got lots to do. I'll still be here when you're done."

I wanted to say something else, or do something to make him more comfortable, but he waved me off. On the way out, I locked the front door and shoved the house keys in my pocket. I headed for the ancient outhouse, opened the wood door with the half-moon on it, and stepped in. The smell gave me a punch in the face that made me think Muhammad Ali or Mike Tyson had hit me in the nose. I tried not to breathe as I lifted the toilet seat and felt along the front of the wood box that made up the seat for the switch. I found it, flipped it, and lifted it as instructed. To my surprise, the entire unit lifted easily until it hit the roof and clicked into place. When the seat and muck had been, there was a stainless-steel ladder that led into the pit.

When I got to the bottom of the shaft, I found a light switch and flipped it up. LED lights came on, illuminating the secret vault that showed my neighbor was a good old-fashioned doomsday prepper. Within the room were shelves stuffed with food, supplies, water, and everything else someone needed to live long term after a nuclear war, a zombie apocalypse, or any other event. In addition to all the supplies were an impressive array of firearms, ammunition, and explosives I didn't trust myself to use.

I traded my old rifle in for an upgrade, complete with a sniper scope and a suppressor, and found three extra magazines and a set of binoculars that I put into a small canvas bag. I selected two revolvers and ammo for each and added them to the bag, along with three grenades that were clearly labeled as stun only, and a large Bowie knife. Satisfied I had enough to get started, I climbed the ladder, put the outhouse back in order, and headed down the trail to my house. A hundred yards before it came into view, I slipped into the woods and moved from tree to tree until my house was in my sights. I dug out the binoculars, dropped to one knee, and scanned my property. I stayed in that position for perhaps forty minutes, and in that time, I spotted four men and a woman, although I had no way of determining who might be in the house, barn, or any of the mobile homes.

When I picked up footsteps behind me, I slowly turned, and since I didn't have the foresight to pull a pistol from my bag, I stayed still, hoping whoever it was would walk right past me.

"Hey!" I whispered when I noticed Kayla strolling right down the driveway.

She stopped when she heard me and looked in my direction. I waved her over, and she joined me by the tree.

"What's going on? Where have you been?" she asked.

"We've got squatters. I've seen five, but there may be more."

"What are we going to do?" Kayla asked.

I didn't answer, and instead passed her a look that answered for me.

"Oh," she said. "Okay. I'm with you, you know that. Do you have a plan?"

"Surprisingly, I do. I plan to move in as close as I can get and then shoot anyone I see."

"What if they hold up in the house?"

I grinned. "I've got a plan for that, too. Let's get closer to the house. Try to walk softly."

With me leading the way, we moved farther down the driveway and tucked ourselves underneath the boughs of a large pine tree. From where we were, the house, one of the mobile homes, and most of the pastureland was well within view. I couldn't view the barn, but I'd take what I could get. I handed Kayla the binoculars and asked her to alert me when she saw someone. The first person she spotted was an overweight man walking slowly to the far side of my property where the stream was. I raised the rifle, ready to shoot while the man was still within my range.

"If you use that, the shot will alert everyone in the house. Are you ready to take that on?" Kayla asked.

I understood her point and handed her the rifle.

"Cover me."

From the bag, I extracted the knife, checked to see if anyone might see me, then started jogging toward the man. I wasn't moving fast, but neither was he, so I covered half of the distance between us in just over a minute. Then I slowed to a fast walk, hoping to silence my approach as much as possible.

I knew once he got to the creek, he would need to climb down the three-foot bank to the water, and I wanted him to be down there when I attacked. Of course, my plan would be immediately foiled if he looked back, or if someone else spotted me from the house, but it was a chance I had to take.

Even at a fast walk, I closed the distance to the man, and got close enough to listen to him humming a song I didn't recognize. I was fifteen feet behind him when I stopped as he did. He swore, then half-slipped, half-lumbered down the bank. I thought he'd look back, but he headed toward the water, which was only a foot away.

I got the knife ready and moved to the bank.

"Hey," I whispered.

When the man started turning around, I jumped from the bank; the knife held out in front of me. I caught the point of the knife right in his neck, two inches below his chin. With the mass of my full body weight behind me, he fell backward into the creek. I fell on top of him, and the knife sliced right through and became stuck in the creek bottom. I got off the man, who was still alive, arms flailing, trying to remove the knife, but he didn't have the strength or the time. A few moments later, he stopped struggling. I had to place my foot on his chest to pull the knife free, then I wiped the blade on his pants, and let him bleed out where he lay.

I looked over the top of the bank, trying to determine if someone saw me. The house and barn remained quiet. I followed the stream until the barn blocked the view of the house, then I jumped up on the bank and ran to the barn. When I reached the front, I realized the padlocks were still fully engaged and figured they hadn't yet found my hiding spot for the keys, but I didn't have them either, so all the resources I had in the barn weren't available to me. I was about to head back to Kayla when I saw a light come on in the mobile home.

I worked my way to the mobile home and peered into the window. There, in my bed on which I slept while I cleaned out the main house, one of the men and the woman I saw were busy getting busy. I left them, then checked the windows of the house.

Inside my house, I spotted one man in the kitchen and two in the living room. Once I finished my reconnaissance, I returned to Kayla's side.

"There are two inside the mobile home bedroom and three in the main house," I said.

"Okay. What's the plan?"

I reached into the bag for the handgun. "My plan is to take out the two making whoopie in my bed, and then we'll clean out the house. There's a chance the ones in the house will catch me, so cover the front door, okay?"

Kayla readied the rifle and took up a position, and I ran from the tree to the mobile home.

I suspected the door would be unlocked, and I was right. Off to my left was a pile of decorative throw pillows I hadn't discarded yet, so I grabbed the top one from the pile and tiptoed to the bedroom. That door was wide open, and before me, the couple was in the missionary position; the man pumping away with all he had. I took a deep breath, stepped into the room and in two smooth motions, placed the pillow on the back of the man's back, pressed the barrel into the pillow, and pulled the trigger. The man jerked, gave the woman one last thrust that was more of a spasm, then laid still. I trained the gun on the woman next, but the life had already passed from her eyes.

I backtracked from the mobile home and had just gotten out of the door when a burly man exited my house. Armed, he aimed at me, and I aimed at him. We both pulled our triggers at the same time, and both of us missed our respective targets. He took a step off the porch with a second man on his heels. The big guy aimed at me again, then spun like a ballerina when Kayla hit him in the shoulder. His friend fired at me, then grabbed his buddy by the shirt and dragged him back inside. I ran back to Kayla.

"Are you hit?" she asked.

"No. Why?"

"Your shirt's full of blood."

I looked down. She was right. "It's not mine. Okay, new plan." I reached into the bag and withdrew two of the grenades. "I'm going to toss these into the window and wait for them to come out."

"Isn't there a back door?"

"Yes."

"Will we be able to cover each door between the two of us?" she asked.

"I don't think we need to. What would you do if you were hanging out in the front and two grenades came in the window?"

"Go out the back?"

I nodded. "That's what I would do, too."

"What do you want me to do?" she asked.

I handed her the grenades. "Can you give me a couple minutes to get to the back, then toss these through the front door?"

She took one from my hand. "Pull the pin and throw?"

"That would be my guess."

Kayla grabbed the other grenade from my hand and left the tree cover. As soon as she did, I ran to the house and stopped at the corner where I'd have cover from the side of the house yet had a superb view of the back door. I counted off the seconds, and only got as far as eighty when I heard two loud booms, one after another, from inside the house. I got down on one knee and waited.

A second later, the man I originally saw in the kitchen came out first. He not only ran from the house, but turned right and rushed toward me. He was two feet away when he spotted me. I saw a gun in his hand, and he tried to raise it in a hurry, but I shot him twice in the chest before he had a chance. By the time he fell, the man I'd wounded ran from the kitchen. He made it three yards, then tripped over his own feet and tumbled into the grass. He rolled over, spotted me, and held out his hands to show me they were empty.

"Don't move!" I shouted at him.

He stayed still as a statue while I crept toward him, wondering where the third man was. As I peered in the kitchen window, I heard two shots from the front of the house.

"Kayla!" I yelled.

I ran around the house and stopped when I got around the corner. The third man I expected to come rushing from the house stood on the porch, then fell. Kayla was already on the ground ten feet from me. I ran to her, dropped to my knees, and took her head in my hands.

"Kayla? Kayla?" I put my fingers against her neck and found a pulse. Then she took a deep breath and opened her eyes.

"That asshole shot me."

EPILOGUE

It turned out the asshole had only winged her. Kayla had taken a round in the shoulder, and it spun her around. She'd fallen, hit her head on the ground, and knocked herself out for a few moments. She'd suffered no worse than a flesh wound and recovered within a couple of days.

By the time I returned to Pops, he had passed. Kayla and I got him on the wagon, and we took him into town. There, the townsfolk gave the well-liked man a proper funeral service and buried him in the church cemetery.

Frank returned the day after we buried Pops, and Dino came around the day after that. Although they live with us now, they both make daily runs up the mountain to Pops' place to check if he'd returned.

When I went back to take care of the man in the backyard, he had disappeared and never returned. The other bodies I dragged to the far side of my property and slid into a deep ravine. The bears, coyotes, raccoons, and all the other critters would eat well for a while.

Once we cleaned up the house and mobile home and removed all traces of the intruders, Kayla and I slipped into the habits of a daily life.

A week after we'd returned, I found Kayla sitting in a lawn chair out in the backyard. Off in the distance, Nutmeg ate the grass in the horse pasture. She wouldn't be alone for long since we planned on adding other horses as soon as we could find them.

"Everything okay?" I asked as I sat down in the empty chair next to Kayla's.

"Yeah. Fine. I'm just tired. It's been a long month."

I didn't argue with that.

"Hey, I've been thinking. See that area just past the gardens?" I said, pointing to the side of Nutmeg's pasture.

"Yeah."

"I imagine that would be a great place to plant those cherry trees. Maybe we could plant apple, peach, and nectarine trees, too."

Kayla smiled. "Sounds great. I make a wicked peach cobbler."

"I love a good cobbler," I said. The peach wasn't my favorite fruit, but I'd hold that information back for now.

We watched Nutmeg in silence for several minutes.

"Baker?"

"Yeah?"

Kayla reached out for my hand, which I gave her without hesitation.

"Thanks for keeping your promise."

"Thanks for calling me. I've thought of you every single day since the last time I saw you."

"You're a good man, Baker."

I shook my head. "Not really. You've seen me do terrible things."

"Things to save us."

I couldn't deny that.

Kayla, not letting go of my hand, got out of her chair and kneeled down before me.

"I love you, Baker."

"I love you, Kayla."

She tipped her head and leaned forward. I took the hint and kissed her. A soft, gentle, lingering kiss. The first kiss. A kiss to remember. A kiss more than a dozen years in the making. We kissed a second time, then she rose and wrapped her arms around me, and I encased her in mine. And for the first time since the world ended, I sensed a new beginning. I was at peace, in love, and I assumed the future was going to turn out just the way we needed it to be.

ABOUT THE AUTHOR

Dan DeKoning was born and raised in Milwaukee, Wisconsin, and currently lives in Knoxville, Tennessee with his wife and their cats.

He is a storyteller and poet who loves to write in a variety of genres and themes. He is also a voracious reader who loves to read anything he can get his hands on.

When he's not writing, you can find him hunting for treasures in used bookstores, or out exploring the planet, or geocaching, or searching for adventures and stories to tell.

ALSO BY DAN DEKONING

This is Dan DeKoning's complete library at the time of publication, but Dan has new books coming out all the time. Sign up for his newsletter at DanDeKoning.com to stay up to date on new releases.

Fiction

Déjà Vu
The Haunting of Hyacinth House
How Deep the Darkness

Geocaching Mystery Series

The Cacheland Conspiracy
The Quincy Bay Quandary
The Secret of the Seven Valleys
The Geocaching Mystery Omnibus – Volume 1

Codi Cassidy Cozy Mystery Series

Acoustics and Alibis
Ballads and Bloodshed
Codas and Calibers
Codi Cassidy Cozy Omnibus – Volume 1

Poetry Collections

Lost and Found
Random Thoughts